Greenie Beani

By

Clayton Crawford

Copyright © 2024 by – Clayton Crawford – All Rights Reserved.

It is not legal to reproduce, duplicate, or transmit any part of this document in either electronic means or printed format. Recording of this publication is strictly prohibited.

Table of Contents

Dedication iv
The Visitor 1
Students 6
Things About The City 11
The Career Of A Girlfriend 13
The Boy Makes A Come Back 16
Sasquiche Sasniche Sings 18
The Sights and Sounds and the Newspaper 23
Great Spiritual Church 27
What My Mom Told Me About Moonsteep 33
Simon-Knight 36
Simon-Knight Part 2 41
Flight to Jeanie Ranch 44
The Jeanie Family 49
Greenie and Beanie 52
Family Time 59
Zomeople 64
Sasquiche Sasniche 66
Greenie on a Yak-Yak-Box 67
A Spiritual Place 73
The Great Spirit Is Calling 75
Beanie 79
Farmsmith Tech-Rancho 82
Without Interdimentional Borders 84
Spirit of Seven Cowboys 89

Madcap Family	95
Spirit of Seven Cowboys	100
"Babadumdum!"	105
Choices We Make, To Fight Fate	107
The Invitation	109
The Towering Inferno	110
A Mother and Daughter	113
A Sheriff and Son	116
The Fire Knights	118
The Fire Knights Part Two	125
A Phyre Battle	127
Battle Ready	132
The News	134
About the Author	138

Dedication

To the Amazing Johnny Strides.... Catch his Vlogs on the Johnny Strides Channel!

To the Amazing people at 3 Coins Morning Restaurant in the City of Richmond Hill located on Yonge Street!

To the Amazing EMS and all Front Line Workers!

To the Amazing People at Amazon Publishing.... Publishing Pros!

The Visitor

(Slip to the Void, Alter Bridge)

"*Bewilder my imagination!*"

The everlasting strange void, Exotic Space, not to be confused with Outer Space.

And what appeared off in the distance within Exotic Space, a Pink Eye resembled an ever-watchful single eye of the Great Spirit. It also contained the Twelve Known Zodiac Multiverses. And, the gap between Verses was measured in Dynyles.

"*A Dynyle is the measurement of the distance between Multiverses,*" Greenie thought. "*Bewilder my imagination,*" she continued thinking, sitting in a dimly lit room surrounded by classmates.

Rouge freely floated with many others, millions and millions, performing a swaying dance, left and right, forward and backward. In a peculiar manner, Rogue and the others resembled a chorus of dancers. The great cosmic dance show.

Rogue stayed in a specific fixed place. According to all the others Rogue was the largest, muscular, bulky. It did not zoom around an elliptical orbit. It had been in the specific spot performing its savvy dance since it was born. Great Spirit had placed Rouge there and, with a flick of her finger, set it into motion, so it believed. Rogue was at the front of all the dancing rocks, a real cosmic rock and roll dance and the smaller one followed its steps.

Those ones performing the elliptical race, they were a family of Planets, a different species, in the Strange Void. It remembered since birth achieving consciousness because layering its cold and dusty surface contained a thin web fiber stretching over it, creating Primordial Memory Rock.

The Family of Planets raced around in elliptical as though the big twins dead center of the Sol-Lar System shining like a pair of candles but also acting as a tether post. The big twins, Apple and Orange, exerted a Mahagick Grasp, never releasing the seven Family of Planets.

The whole group of planets was nicknamed, the Spirit of Seven Cowboys and each given a name blessed by the Great Spirit. *"The names of these worlds will be everlasting throughout multiverses,"* the Voice of Great Spirit remarked.

Rouge's Memory Rock certainly remembered the hand of the Great Spirit, placing him specifically in his dancing orbit. *"Rouge, one day, your dancing will trigger events that are not your fault. Do not feel guilty; feel free to dance. I am giving you this gift of the dance. It's part of my plan,"* Great Spirit's voice whispered across the fathoms of space.

"What will happen to me, will I die?"

"Unfortunately, in your current stony body, yes, but I give you my word; your spirit, your rock and roll spirit, will be with me. I will return your spirit to someone I have chosen, and you will help this person become a rock for many ages, and one day if all goes as planned become Fire Knight," Great Spirit explained.

One day, a mighty energy blast smacked Rouge. The dancing orbit was popped at the moment like a balloon and just as air rushing out of a balloon, it deflated. It kick-started the beginning of a new birth. The family of planets felt the vibes, and they twitched in personal orbits. *"Slow down, Jamie!"* ... *"Omar, use your air volcanoes to brake!"*... *"Kidney, you are the largest of all us, use your great love to shelter all of us!"* ... *"Sheranda, you are Kidney's favorite, a nurse, so help us in our time of need!"* ... *"Garrick, you are the mortal angel cowboy with the wings, painted by Great Spirit on your back... Forever the angel that does not fly, but this time, you need to grow wings to possess a full-size mustard seed of faith in the Great Spirit!"* ... *"Bianca, Ford, you are teenage lovers, the youngest of all of us, our offspring; we pray you survive and nurture younger worlds!"*

Tumbling through the Strange Void, the velocity of speed started getting faster and faster. Rogue wondered if Apple and Orange had smacked its body with a baseball bat, a grand slam.

Rogue's body started rumbling, and dust created a long fiery tail, a dragon's tail and bits of rock chipped off. The Primordial Memory Rock, the web fibers no longer cohesive and no longer absorbing information the way they once did, and so, Rogue, at the last minute, felt Soul-Rock had been set free by Great Spirit. She kept her promise. She did not want Rogue to feel guilty, "*Great Spirit, have I performed well? Please tell me, I am scared!*"

"*Rogue, you are with me, and you have performed your celestial dancing, entertaining me. Do not look at what is about to happen; it's not your fault. I will release you into the heart of the body of the chosen one. I also have others chosen in a future battle,*" Great Spirit admitted.

"*Why will there be a battle?*"

"*Rouge, you must keep this a secret, like a rock.*"

"Yessem. I can do that; keep a secret in my heart of rock and roll."

"Former King Baal of all the continent, Zeus, evolved into the Arezon-Knysght taping in the energy Primordial Phyre and waged war upon Taprobane Island, accompanied by the Legions of Creatures of Phyre. Arezon-Knysght was struck down and defeated. The first time, a sword sliced through his heart of hate. His body has been found by a species, the Amemga and they have resurrected the Arezon-Knysght. A future battle will soon be on Taprobane Island," Great Spirit explained. "The chosen one is part of my bloodline," she added.

Students

(Another Brick in the Wall Part 2, The Wall – Pink Floyd)

Present Day

14th Frump/ Vamphyre 8412 AKP (After King Pyre-Lyre Phyre)

Zerth – Planet 2023

The odor lingering in the classroom was spring pleasant.

"*Mister Elfant enjoys scents*," Greenie Beanie Jeanie thought. Her eyes focused on the monitor. It showed the history lesson of how the old world, Pentateuch, got destroyed just a little more than ten thousand years ago when an asteroid smashed into Shadow-Face. "*Bewilder my imagination*," she thought, gasping upon seeing the rouge asteroid smashing the second satellite, Shadow-Face. At the conclusion of the lesson, the last image showed remnants of a fractured moon, chunks of space rock that could at any time be jarred loose and come crashing down upon the world once again. The survivors of the old world now call it Zerth. "*Great Spirit has chapter dedicated to the Twelve Multiverses and various solar systems where planets exist, teaming with life*," she thought, and then a hand touched her hand. Quickly, she panned her head left to see the trimmed face of Sasquiche Sasniche. "Is a Tootbug dancing up one of your nostrils?" she asked with an accusing tone. Next, she purposely allowed him to keep his fingers on the top side of her hand. Perhaps she was afraid to pull away because Greenie really did not want to shrug off a friend. "*Bewilder my imagination*," she continued thinking, gasping in shock upon seeing the rouge asteroid smashing the second satellite, Shadow-Face. It replayed in her mind.

Sasquiche smiled in response, deep down in him, he could never find a reason to be angry or get irked by the way she spoke. Oh, sure, they talked up a storm, and perhaps that might be squabble, but it would never spill over to the next day.

The classroom lights came on.

The students began murmuring among themselves quietly discussing what they watched. It did not scare them to death, but it shocked them awake. The previous world had come to a fiery brimstone end by a chunk of smash rock colliding with the satellite Shadow-Face as the indigenous people named it. The documentary showed in graphic detail how Shadow-Face splintered and fractured and how a single chunk with many bits of rock forever altered their world.

"The Astro-Walkers call this Great Spirit's Fastball if any of you enjoy the sport Baseball," Mr Elfant remarked, making his way from the rear of the class to the front. He wore the traditional History sandals, tailored pants, and a belt, and the upper portion was a The Big Sweater with bold letters PH, short for Professor of History. "Does anyone here know the Astro-Walker who said these famous words, 'Great Spirit threw a mighty fastball and shattered Shadow-Face!" He gazed upon his students.

Sasquiche raised his hand quickly. He blurted. "Oscar Grapevine! He was the first Zerthling to step out onto the lunar surface on the rock called Chocolate Chip during the first mission on 3rd Moonday, Mahagick 8062, fifteen years ago. The rock actually resembles a chocolate chip cookie broken in half, rough around a portion. Our neighbor country, Phyre, was where the first lift-off took place, at 15:23 hours pm on the Island of Taprobane, but not the mythical Taprobane Island where Great Spirit resides., the country of Phyre is also home to our King Pyre-Lyre Phyre, and our country, Zeus is part of the twenty-five countries under the Commonwealth of Zerthlings. We are one people with mixed race. And that's a smart idea. Oscar Grapevine is a Phyre-Man, as those from the country of Phyre like to be called. King Pyre-Lyre is Pumpskin, and that is slang for being a colored person. Me and Greenie were born fifteen years ago," he said speaking quickly and apparently all in one breath.

Classmates sat dead silent.

Sasquiche looked around, scratching his head, puzzled, seeing various expressions. He turned his attention to Greenie, and at first, she hesitated and finally whispered.

"Your information flew over their heads like a hot air balloon."

Sasquiche smiled proudly, folding his arms across his chest. He completely understood. He conquered.

The school bell shrilled.

The sudden distraction woke everyone up.

"Enjoy the Spirit of Seven Cowboys long weekend, everyone and don't forget to read your book for homework. I want book reports on my desk pronto, chapters four, five and six all about Zomeople race, when you return on Moonday," Mr Elfant said while watching the students gathered paraphernalia, the Digital Pocket-Book, but he noticed how Greenie used a utility belt and clipped her school device to it. "Let me see," he asked, stepping forward. "Digital Pocket-Books don't come with a clamp or clip. Did you invent this?" he asked.

Greenie nodded in a confident gesture. "Absolutely, Mr Elfant," she responded with an enthusiastic punchline. "Fire Knights use utility belts to hold specific equipment. The belts have pockets containing tools of their Fire Knight Trade, communication, the Mahagick Bow and laser arrow, the Mahagick Pistol, Mahagick Whip, and other stuff. This student Gizmo did not have a clamp, and so I super glue and attach this clamp to the backside, and now it is safe on my belt," Greenie explained as fourteen-year-old inventor.

A tall girl with goth dark hair draped at the sides and parted in the middle impatiently tapped Greenie's shoulder for attention. She also was sporting a cultural Garnet crystal dead center of her forehead. It stayed there, held in position by the power locked inside her mind. On the left bicep was a secondary cultural tattoo, but at this stage of her life, it was a special marker that would not wash away so quickly in a shower. Once every two or three weeks, Winnykneebee Salavamp required new ink to be applied. She trusted Greenie to apply the correct amount of ink to make it appear magical.

"Ms Salavamp," Mr Elfant said, slightly offended because he was speaking to Greenie. "Greenie, King Pyre Phyre will show up at the Spirit of Seven Cowboys. He wants to meet young people who share his birthday, giving out invitations," he remarked.

"Me? Mine is sixteenth Tuesday, Vamphyre born 8077," she blurted.

Winnykneebee Salavamp stood for a moment and then decided to wander around the classroom.

"Fire Knights use a form of Mahagick Primordial Particles or MPPs establishing not plasma, but Primordial Phantasm energy.

The Phantasm energy is what powers the Evergreen Swords and enables them to fight the Phyre, not to be confused with regular fire. Phyre is an ancient dime-god creature, being, beast, whatever: former King Baal is a perfect example of a dime-god and/or based conjecture and myth," Greenie said.

"Hold that thought, it's time for you to get underway, go and enjoy the long weekend," Mr Elfant chortled.

Winnykneebee quickly reached out to Greenie, tugging on a hand. The girls ran out of History Class.

Things About The City

(Age of Aggression – Skyrim cover -- Malukah)

A flock of Screecher-Owls flew over the Spirit of 7 Cowboys as they performed this flight of fancy in the afternoon. They had an average wingspan, and their chests, the males, were titan red, obviously to attract and woe the female counterparts. Only the alpha female would fly next to her alpha male at the head of the flock while the other females were back attending to the offspring. The female Screecher-Owl was smaller and sometimes would piggyback on her mate, but always with wings open to help navigate. It was obvious within the Screecher-Owl community there existed a higher-achy.

"Long weekend!" young voices shouted as students from Spirit of 7 Cowboys all-age school. The largest educational center in the area contains a population of five thousand students with overcrowding in classrooms; the change was needed, and action was to build a new school. A large patch of soil to the left had a fence surrounding the lot and construction bulldozers and digging equipment parked inside. No one was sure what could happen, perhaps another mall. OMG!

A group of rowdy parents stood on a corner with signs: **NEW SCHOOL NEEDED, NOT A SHOPPING MALL!** The Spirit of Seven Cowboys News Crews from various news agencies sat inside a buggy cabin. It was pulled up pulled by Hopperhorses. The Driver pulled on the reins and gave a bark of a command, "Stop!" He pulled on the reigns, giving a physical signal. The Hopperhorses obeyed. Reporters scrambled out of the cabin. Simultaneously, the hand-held electronic devices.

One of the reporters aimed the recording device and captured the flock of Screecher-Owls in flight of fancy. They whooshed left and then right, performed in unison a full midair loop like a roller coaster and then returned to a regular flight pattern.

"*Dumb-Bats are much more acrobatic than Screech-Owls,*" Greenie thought in a cocky tone. She shifted her body, adjusting the backpack. It wasn't heavy or awkward, just a nuisance. "*My pet Dumb-Bat, Corkey-Dorkey, can fly circles, swan dives and steep dives and loops around those ass-hat Screecher-Owls,*" she continued thinking.

The Career Of A Girlfriend

(Life is a Highway, Tom Cochrane)

Piercing sirens ripped the air—Cherry red EMS cylindrical tankers displaying bold name: **Fire Stormers**. The Spirit of Seven Cowboys city council permitted EMS vehicles to harness powerful souped engines to help the brave men and women race to a fire within a few minutes. The exhaust pipes spewed a stew of fumes, operating on delinquency, drunken diesel energy.

Greenie accompanied Winnykneebee across the street toward Seven Park. *"It's not so much the sound that is the challenge, and it's the odorous, funky fumes of the Fire Storm engines. My jet pack does not reek like rotting bananas or milk because I designed it harnessing Mahagick Elements to let me fly,"* she continued thinking. It wasn't the seventh park, and the city council had decided to give it that particular name. And, although a solid four inches shorter, her legs managed to move quickly enough, keeping in pace with her taller friend who had a steady, longer stride. Her piercing eyes caught some dude doing something that made her blood boil, and she stopped midway across the street, gawking.

A cigarette was flicked onto the sidewalk. The red amber flickered one last time until a thick sole black boot squished it, smothering the fire. A whiff of smoke lingered. The boots walked over to a Hopperhorse. The person hopped on the saddle in a single step up. The person wore a cucullus draping the face. The person was typical of men, a Hearty Coat, all-weather designed. He used his knee to jab it against the Hopperhorse and pulled on the reins, steering the animal in the direction he wanted to go.

Winnykneebee spun around, everything moving in slow motion, and with both hands snatched Greenie out of the danger of being trampled by a Hopperhorse pulling a buggy. Heart rate amped up a few notches. At one point, Winnykneebee nearly lost her footing, but miraculously, she felt something prevent her from wildly spinning out of control, a ghostly hand perhaps from the Great Spirit. The Hopperhorses reared up right in front of both girls as the Driver shouted commands to stop.

Pedestrians skedaddled out of the way.

A Skunsquirrel zoomed across the street at that moment and ran underneath a shrub.

Winnykneebee pulled her short friend across the street to safety within the confines of Seven Park.

A ghost breath of wind shook the Twig Trees and Squiggle Trees of Seven Park. People in the park looked around, puzzled, they stood absolutely still, and the crying of an infant became quiet and changed to a giggle, perhaps tickled by the ghost wind that had whooshed up and fell silent.

"Do you bug in the brain!?" someone shouted.

Street Cleaners used vacuums to suck up Hopperhorse manure decorating the road. The vacuum device was attached to their back. The hoses were long enough to keep a distance from the manure. Some wore masks, some did not, personal choice. It was a dirty job, but people needed to work to pay bills, food, rent, laundry and perhaps go on a date.

The after-school traffic consisted of various buggies. Each buggy could fit no more than fifty students. Those kids were from about Spirit of Seven Cowboys, enclaves and the inner city nooks and crannies, so shipping them home was easy. And the buggies were decorated in bright yellow distinguishing them. The Drivers sitting up top in the navigation station all wore a dull grey Union Uniform, and a patch displayed the Union symbol.

The Hopperhorses produced various burp sounds communicating with one another or a stomp of their foot in another form of communication.

The Boy Makes A Come Back

(The Terminator Soundtrack - Burning In The Third Degree)

"Greenie! Greenie!" the Voice of a boy shouted.

Winnykneebee held both sides of Greenie's arms, shocked by what had happened. "Do you bug in the brain!?"

Greenie shook her head no. "Some dude just flicked his smoke. He could not put inside a designated street tray for smoke-butts," she admitted, "his actions totally roasted my mind," she added.

"Whoa," Winnykneebee remarked. "My eyes did not see any such dude," she confessed and released her friend. Crossing her arms while standing and looking at the expression her friend wore, she, too, made an expression. "Greenie, you need to focus your mind on the present. I might not be there the next time to save your butt," she said.

Greenie scratched her head. "Yeah. I know."

"Greenie! Greenie!" the Voice of a boy shouted.

"Hey, watch it, kid, you're going to get yourself run over by a Hopperhorse!"

"Kid, you just stepped into a pile of manure."

"Tell me something I don't know."

"Don't be in such a flurry!"

"Right! But, I am in a hurry!" the boy managed to negotiate get across the street. He reached an arm and tapped Greenie's shoulder. She spun around with a shocked expression. "Are you hurt?"

"Sasquiche!" Greenie responded simultaneously.

Three other girls hurried over from a park picnic table.

Sasquiche Sasniche Sings

(Heart of Courage -Two Steps From Hell)

Seven minutes later.

Greenie sat with Winnykneebee and several girls at Seven Park at a picnic table across the street from the school fifteen minutes later. Sasquiche decided to hang out. "*Sasquiche Sasniche, his Bloodline lived in the Ocean Forest, a whole other world, but his people are considered Backwoodsman, eccentric ideas how about technology terrorizing their tranquil environment*," she thought.

"You know, there is a song about a girl in the Great Spirit Book, in the section, Rock Psalms," Bubblegum said, chewing a wad of gum.

"I know the song," Sasquiche blurted.

"Does the Sasquatch bloodline believe in the Great Spirit?" Doublegum spat out a sarcastic question.

Sasquiche blinked twice. He scrunched a face. "Just because my people live in the Ocean Forest doesn't mean we are Neanderthals!" he countered with both hands resting on his hips. "King Pyre Phyre has destroyed one hundred thousand hectares of forest to resettle a vast portion of Vamphyre City. Although Ocean Forest is an ocean of swamps, bogs, rivers, ponds and hidden lakes, it's still a vital resource for all of Zerth," he said with a mouthful.

"I wasn't trying to offend you."

"I am proud to be a Backwoodsman."

Greenie's eyes opened wide with surprise. "Sasquiche, how would you know Psalm Fourteen?" she asked, taking over the conversation. "It's my favourite Psalm. The character is named after me," she giggled. "Great Spirit has a real sense of humor," she added.

"Can you sing?" Rumblegum asked.

"I am in Sasquatch choir!" Sasquiche boasted, pointing two thumbs toward himself confidently.

The triple sisters exchanged expressions and then turned their attention toward Winnykneebee and then Greenie. The girls cast a glare at the boy.

"If you want to belong to our All-Sisters Club," Winnykneebee said, "you gotta sing," she explained.

"Today?"

"Yup."

"Right now."

"This very second?"

Greenie stepped forward, holding Sasquiche's hands, keeping them from trembling. "Sing for me, you brave guy," she encouraged and batted her eyes, flirting.

Sasquiche cast an expression at all the girls. He sized up the situation. He shrugged. "Sure. I will sing so as you promise I can belong to the All-Sisters Club."

"Uhhh, I am not sure," Bubblegum said, narrowing her brows. "I wonder how a guy can or should belong to the All-Girls Club?"

"I don't make those big decisions," Doublegum admitted, chewing gum. She blew a bubble, and it popped with a ***smack!***

"You demand a lot, Little Man," Rumblegum remarked, crossing her arms across her chest.

Winnykneebee snapped her fingers as a seed of an idea plopped into her imagination, a super duper sensation. "A partnership."

"Sasquiche can be my date," Greenie said firmly, hooking her arm around his right arm.

"Sing," Winnykneebee and the triplets encouraged.

Sasquiche drew a breath and exhaled slowly enough to regulate his breathing.

Chapter One: Greenie's Song

'There was a girl, Greenie Beanie Jeanie

And she lived on Zerth, a very different planet-earth

There was a girl, Greenie Beanie Jeanie

And she lived on a farm tending to goat-cows, frog-pigs, and other things

She lived outside the Spirit of Seven Cowboys

The homestead of happiness, a Dumb-Bat for a pet

One day she would choose the name, Shalloween-Scream'

The All-Sisters Club stepped back, thrown off guard, while simultaneously staring at Sasquiche Sasniche, listening to his voice. It was caramel, a real smoothie, gourmet. His voice sounded therapeutic, tugging their hearts, evoking a consistency that which only being blessed by a higher authority, the Great Spirit of Multiverse.

"Spooky," Winnykneebee commented. She touched the Garnet Stone necklace, drawing on it supernatural power for inner strength. "Adorable," she added.

"Shalloween-Scream is a shadowy character in the Great Spirit Book," Bubblegum said. "It's a story about a girl who becomes mentored by a Fire Knight of compassion, intelligence, wit and endurance. Shalloween-Scream shortens the name to Shallowscream. The word 'Shalloween' originates from the ancient Kingdom of Baal, which hailed from Vamphyre City. Shalloween was a daughter of Baal, the Vamphyre King who indulged in Dark Mahagick and adopted the name, Arezon-Knysght. Winnykneebee is a young Mahagick person, like me and my sisters," she explained.

"None of the All-Sisters will ever play with Dark Mahagick; that's what King Baal did, and he became the Arezon-Knysght," Winnykneebee said in a confident tone. "I am Vamphyre; my family bloodline originates from that ancient city," she added, gesturing to her Goth cultural clothing.

"Shallowscream, it's an ancient expression 'can you not hear the woeful cries of children'," Sasquiche quoted. Next, he withdrew a bottle of water from his knapsack and chugged all of it, feeling dehydrated. He proudly burped. He saw the girls shake their heads disapproving. "I need to go home, a hot air balloon," he added and stepped forward. "Greenie, call me?" he asked and then walked away smiling, leaving the All-Girls Club mystified, puzzled, perplexed and dumbfounded. He knew he had them in the palm of his hand. *"Singing always soothes the souls of girls, something my Father and older Brother taught me,"* he thought.

The Sights and Sounds and the Newspaper

(Soak Up The Sun, Sheryl Crow)

"So, Winnykneebee and the Triplet Sisters have invited me to Lucifer City to catch a show, to listen to the Multiverse Group, Super Assassins," Greenie thought as she wandered through Seven Park. "*In one week, I will be traveling by train to Lucifer City; that should be extremely fun*," she continued thinking in a happy-go-lucky mood. Stepping out of the park at one of five exit points, she could see signs stretching over Cowboy Avenue; the main strip of the city banners read: **Spirit of Seven Cowboys 245 Years – Parade – Come Everyone**. "*It's not the first time at the parade, but that won't happen until Soondee, noonish time*," she continued thinking while standing at a crosswalk. "*Better pay attention as Winnykneebee recommended*," she continued thinking. "*Mom and Dad will be expecting me home by dinner, so don't wander the city too much. Exploring is an adventure, just like wandering the farm in the village of Little Cowboy*," she continued thinking and continued walking across the street when the light turned green.

"Ladies and Gentlemen of Spirit of Seven Cowboys, I am your Mayor. These people are your council members. We work hard every day to serve you, great people. It's an honor to serve the people. Tomorrow, on Sumzee and Soondee, this urban city will engage in a festival of events. Be prepared for a parade, several floats, and all the snacks, and there will be games."

Greenie could see a crowd at the bottom steps of City Hall listening to the speech. She decided to step in and listen to the Mayor, "*It would be rude not to pay attention to our Mayor because, as our Mayor, he might say something intelligent, and he might need someone like me to volunteer for a mission to help others. A Fire Knight goes on missions to help other, but they also travel in a Fire Knight Troop,"* she thought, and her attention turned upward, seeing four school-designated zeppelins floating overhead.

The outer shell had ringlets of orange, identifying them as school airships. Each one could hold as many as three hundred students, and they were taking them home to various towns in places that were too rough for vehicles to go so easily. *"Riding inside a Zep is eyebrow-raising, the sprawling landscape is beautiful, and the trees look so small from a bird's eye view. Sasquiche and I take the same Zep. Perhaps that's why he showed up; maybe he wanted me to ride with him, but nowadays I fly to and from home using my jet-pack,"* she thought.

"Move, bub, that's my seat!" Big Bull demanded, standing in the aisle. He wore a Slayer-Jacket, made of Halfbutt, a young Fatbutt creature. Fully grown a Fatbutt had four horns and a large crumpled head, ugly or scary or adorable depending on a person's point of view. The oval eyes were placed at the sides of the head, enabling it to see behind and, therefore, giving it an edge over natural predators and hunters.

"Do you own this fleabag contraption, Big Bull?" Sasquiche demanded, sitting in a zeppelin full of students. He knew there was enough space to share the seat. He decided to play the game.

"Yes, I do."

"Show me the receipt."

"It's at home."

"Go home and get the receipt and show me the receipt and then I will move," Sasquiche said and provoked the three other boys hanging around Big Bull to laugh.

"Who do you think you are, a stand-up comedian?"

"No. No! I am sit-down comedian, and I am a singer."

"A singer. Then sing for us," Freaky-Hair encouraged.

"I sing for girls, that's free, but for you four, it will cost big bucks."

"Boys, we are in flight mode, find a seat," the stewardess said, approaching them. "Young man, would you mind sharing the seat?"

Sasquiche shifted closer to the window. He made a gesture to Big Bull. The other boys sat in other seats nearby.

When the stewardess walked away, that was the opportunity Big Bull needed and grabbed Sasquiche by his collar.

"Are you looking for a bruising?"

Sasquiche smiled, a big, fat, cheesy smile. "Are you looking for a lawsuit, criminal code against bullying, three to five years on probation and including the possibility of time inside a detention center. Maybe some inmate will give you a butt ride. And perhaps, but in so much as psychological damage to me, the therapy sessions and, therefore, your parents will be paying my parents big bucks!"

Big Bull released the prey. He shifted in his seat, uncomfortable for a moment, realizing the prey was pretty smart, perhaps a smart-aleck. There was no Smart-Alec Degree, no Masters or PhD, just a punch in the nose, but not right now. Later.

A minute passed.

Big Bull started laughing.

"What's so funny?"

"Sasquiche, you make me laugh," Big Bull admitted, rubbing his beard thoughtfully. "We're both Backwoods people; our forest is our friend. You're in the Big Bull Squad. But, you need to pay attention to a couple of rules," he added.

"Which are?"

"My Dad is one of the Sheriffs of Spirit of Seven Cowboys, so we cannot break the law," he remarked, "and number two, written in the Great Spirit Book, there is a verse... Be Humble... Be Patient... Be Willing to Learn. Got it?"

"Sounds like a cool concept. I accept your terms of belonging to Big Bull Troop," Sasquiche agreed and performed the classic High-Five. "And I just got accepted in Winnykneebee's all-girl troop," he added as the three Triplet Brothers gawked at him, astonished.

A giant pair of spinning fans gave the dirigible the ability to steer against the wind. It also had a pair of puff-exhaust ports; combined, they spat out a push force to nudge against the wind. The Tinkermen Inc. understood how to build machines.

Great Spiritual Church

(Hawkmoon 269, U2)

Greenie walked about, but she did not need to walk far from Seven Park to hear powerful Rock-Evangelistic music playing from Great Spirit Church. Curious, she jogged across the street, dodging Hopperhorses pulling buggies. And once, on the other side of the street, she ran up the steps and went inside the church.

"The Great Spirit Church in Spirit of Seven Cowboys is open all day and all night, never to close its doors for those who feel need shelter and food. Mom and Dad have always encouraged me if I get lost in the city, always to come here and I can call home, and they can find me and bring me home. This place is really, really fun to hang out from time to time," Greenie thought as she went through the foyer and entered the main building.

Greenie's attention was captured by the various images. On the western interior wall, an illustrator and painter had painted a massive stone wall, and people kneeling and worshipping, and the exterior of the wall, soldiers of an army attempting to knock it down with tools by the fabled warrior Moon Wolfphyre, but the wall would not buckle, the rock could not be chipped, and it would never fall. *"The Great Spirit Wall, made by the legendary Mahagick Person named Troy Wall and its foundation is built on the Faith Soil. Moon Wolfphyre and his Arm of Demons could never destroy the western wall,"* she continued thinking and walking about a bit more.

Greenie, looking to the eastern interior wall of Great Spirit Church and again another painting showing a collage, Fire Knights Troop on winged horses, soaring over a battle, or on landing on the battlefield fighting creatures or standing in a field with the horses. Their facial expressions showed battle expressions, a scar or two, a boldness, and an attitude. The battles they engaged in were the blessings of the Great Spirit. "*It is written Great Spirit Bible, the original Fire Knights, twelve of them in total, each one came from the Twelve Zodiac Multiverse, one from each verse. Great Spirit hand-picked each Fire Knight because they had a pure heart, and in time, on the battlefield, they could wage a battle similar to the Spartans. It is written the Spartans considered them brothers and sisters sent to them from a faraway island because they helped the Spartans win the freedom of a land called Greece. The Fire Knights honor, prayer and willingness to help those who are in need of protection from tyrants. Great Spirit wrote in verse, 'Fire Knights are my Everlasting Candle, and my wax slows to melt, a beacon in the ebony of emptiness, a lighthouse',*" she continued thinking.

"May I help you?" a voice asked.

Greenie spun around, startled and saw Sister Spirit wearing a hooded robe of all-white and a glowing purple crystal necklace.

"Greenie Beanie Jeanie. What a pleasant and wonderful surprise you have returned to the Great Spirit Church. Are you enjoying your adventures! Are you cold? Are you in need of shelter? Are you hungry?" Sister Spirit asked with eyes opening wide. Standing up and shouting, announcing with glee. "Everyone, Greenie has returned!"

The band on stage stopped playing. One by one, the band members came off the stage, approaching Greenie.

People from every nook and cranny of the building came out of hiding, one could say, and they approached gradually.

"I did not come here to cause such a fuss," Greenie admitted, stepping back two feet, puzzled at the adult attitude, "the music intrigued me. I am in that pocket age, teenhood. The musicians are truly super assassins with instruments of spiritual mass destruction. I really, really, really groove to the hyperactive spiritual music, super assassins," she confessed to the people around her.

"Hello, Greenie!" Brother Spirit said, opening his arm wide. And they embraced.

"Greenie likes our music group. She suggested the name Super Assassins," a second Spirit Sister remarked.

"Super Assassins," Brother Spirit repeated, intrigued, rubbing his chin.

"Sabertooth!" Greenie exclaimed as if something inside her tickled her brain, and a flood of memories burst out. She sized up the purple-skinned man, muscular, not far beyond his prime and powerful arms. "Sabertooth. You are truly a warrior of many worlds in a spectrum of verses. The Poorest Army of Great Spirit would eagerly follow you into the ebony of all battles to save a single spirit!"

He chuckled in response. "Flattering as always." He sized her up, all four feet five inches. "Your comment just a moment ago, 'the Poorest Army of Great Spirit'... You are reciting a verse in Great Spirit Book, Book 5, Friends and Foes."

"I don't mean to show off. I am sorry. But am I reciting a verse? Bewilder my imagination," Greenie responded, puzzled, placing a palm against her forehead. Her mind tingled.

"'And there came a time when the Poorest Army of Great Spirit stood up against Moon Wolfphyre and slay down the wicket creatures of disease thought and serpent tongues drawing upon free will, and Great Spirit blessed the poorest army by giving them invisible windshields and umbrellas so neither stinging acid rain nor spit of snakes' mouths. Mahagick battle boots and bows and arrows were given to the Poorest Army making them invincible. Wolfphyre, realizing the power of the Great Spirit Poorest Army and how they had not lost a single soldier in battle, re-called his creature army to retreat to the caves of Arezon-Knysght in a land of stench and death, but his army, fortunately, had been cut to one-third of its original size by the Poorest Army'. The Poorest Army on that day rescued one hundred and forty-four thousand abducted souls," Sabertooth recited from memory.

People listened to Sabertooth's words. They could see Greenie listening intently but also showing puzzlement. People around her exchanged expressions with one another.

"Would you like our Humble Band to play you a song, one song, just for you," Roy McCoy asked. I am the lead vocalist."

"Sure! That would be fantastic!" Greenie said with eyes wide open, showing happiness. "Roy, re-name the group," she spat out in an unconscious manner.

"What would you suggest?"

"Super Assassins, a spiritual rock progressive group that never misses its musical target. And one day, the Super Assassins will play in the biggest cities," she said.

The Four Members exchanged expressions and gradually warmed up to the suggestion.

"The Super Assassins," one of the players repeated.

"Come on guys, let's perform a song for Greenie!" the Drummer agreed and gestured for bandmates to follow.

"The Super Assassins," the Fourth Player repeated as if hypnotized.

Greenie sat in a pew and listened to a single song with Spirit Sister and friends of the Great Spirit Church.

Chapter Two: Greenie's Song

A train ride from the town of Spirit of Seven Cowboys

Sharing an adventure with friends, a jet pack adventure, flight for a spirit Stretching across the landscape, a wild whoooohoooo ride looking out through the train window A sprawling tundra landscape, mountains with snow peaks Blinding spiritual sunlight glistening off Greenie Beanie Jeanie and friends arrive in Lucifer City Smokestacks rising and turning the blue sky pale, belching a froth like a hacking cough Vehicles flying about like insects, horns honking, the screaming of sirens Greenie's mind brewing with the toxicity of adventure, swirling Maaaaaaaaaadness!

Greenie's friends helped her over to a park bench, catching her breathing

The city sick, drunken on toxic fumes, mind-numbing

The Humble Band stopped playing. They could see Greenie had disappeared.

Spirit Sister stood up, eyes searching for Greenie. "She... She was just here a moment ago."

"Where did Greenie go off to?" another person asked.

"Greenie was here."

"Was Greenie here in the Great Spirit Church?"

"My mind is numbing," Spirit Brother Sabertooth admitted, pressing his fingers against his temples.

"Quickly, search every room. Was Greenie ever really here in the Church?" Spirit Sister asked.

What My Mom Told Me About Moonsteep

"It would be nice to become a Fire Knight, men and women working to help others. They travel to many worlds within the Twelve Zodiac Multiverses. They use Mahagick Pistols similar to the Moonsteep Street Surgeons, doctors without Multiverse Borders. The Fire Knights have a variety of tools of the trade. But, I think Mom wishes me to become a Street Surgeon because she always allows me to learn about the tools she uses during situations. She is no longer traveling to various worlds, now, she lives on the Jeanie Farm and operates a medical business stretching around the Country of Zeus... Yapa-yapa-yapa.

The planet Moonsteep can be defined as a world unlike any other I can imagine; maybe not that strange, but it's located in the Firefly constellation. It has seven planets in the solar system with three Jupiter Classified worlds, and all three shield it from rouge asteroids that could annihilate the world. Zerth got clobbered. The people of Moonsteep, therefore, had time to evolve into a world dedicated to serving other worlds, bringing the knowledge of medicine and teachings about mind, body and soul. The Moonsteep Medical Empire currently spans as many as, but perhaps not quite one million worlds, spanning across the Twelve Zodiac Multiverses.

Moonsteep is Pangaea, but there is a single large island, Manlantean. Mom is Eknakamoonknoon with Zebra people and Tall Ones, like my Mom, who is extraordinarily tall and has a long neck. My Mom has told me that Zebra people can shape-shift their facial features, which my Grandpa can perform, but Grandma cannot. Grandpa is much shorter, human-like like Dad, but Grandma is super tall like Mom and Aarat, the older brother who keeps on stretching. He is nearly six foot eight. And Moonsteep is *a mixed race, Dewskinners, Aquaskin, Eknakamoonknoon, Talloween, Manlantean, and the Indigenous Swamp Nation people... Yapa-yapa-yapa.*

Oh gosh, I got that silly expression stuck on my tongue. Gross!

The Country of Eknakamoonknoon, which I learned through oral stories told to me by cousins, aunts and uncles and my grandparents and photos, and a talking Moonsteep Paradog... Yapa-yapa-yapa.... It contains smooth plains in the south, a green world, and a wheat basket capable of feeding millions. Mountains are in the north and along the border of Bog Nation. Swamp Nation is at the most southern end of the Pangaea landscape and is treacherous. Eknakamoonknoon is the largest land nation with the longest sea border and kisses the Emmaga Border. The Emmaga Border is extremely mountainous, misty, foggy and mysterious, with many mythical stories... Yapa-yapa-yapa.

Stop with that silly expression. This is what happens with superior brain power, an expression from childhood: a kernel pops in my neurons, and then another kernel pops and –gross!

Mom has taught me many of the tools of the Street Surgeon Tradecraft, the MMD is the Mahagick Medical Device, capable of analyzing thousands of viruses from multiverses. She showed me how it worked, and we both participated in Hologram scenarios with fake people, but the instrument helped me learn about various viruses. Yeah, I truly believe my Mom wants me to go off to Hammurabi University on Moonsteep and become a Street Surgeon.

The Street Surgeons emerged on Moonsteep during the Virus War. After the first pandemic threatened to wipe out Pangaeains, that's the real name of the planet, and there was a century lull in the battle and nature returned with a vengeance, unleashing the Stepstrepho-Mexophleghm virus. It was like a thief in the night and broad daylight. But, those who would be the first Street

Surgeons had learned resilience, never to complacent and rose to the challenge to wage a war against Stepstrepho-Mexophleghm... Those merger fifteen hundred men and women, scientists with a touch of military warrior mindset, and they dared to go out into the streets to inoculate tens of thousands around the Pangaea landscape. Those scientists were watchful guardians and earned the official title, Street Surgeons and became the backbone of the Moonsteep Medial Empire.

But, I live here; my world has suffered, reborn as the ebony ashes of the Phyrebyrd, and we, as Zerthling, are resilient in our own unique way. The ancient world called this world, Pentateuch and the world before that, Eden, and the world before that Tree and the very first world called this world, Seed. Hhhhmmmm!? How do I know all the stuff? Oh, Mom must have told me during a bedtime story.

Music best discovered over my Faraway Frequency Radio, honing in on song played on the Zilohertz Frequency."

"Where am I?" Greenie wondered and stopped walking.

Simon-Knight

(Bits and Pieces, Day Clark Five)

Greenie returned to Seven Park. She strolled up to the locker zone and, using a key twisted it opening the door. It swung open. Removing the knapsack, she put it down at her feet and next reached inside the locker, taking out a jet pack. She leaned against the lower lockers. Next, she removed the jet pack bomber jacket. She slipped it on. It fit snugly. It was given to her Father. *"Dad and Uncle helped me build this following the instructions, powered by Mahagick Particles emanating from the Zilohertz crystal group. The Zilohertz orange crystal power my flight pack is,"* she thought, slipping her arms through the sleeve holes.

"Hold on a sec!" a baritone voice shouted. "You are not doing it right." A man approached, and he helped adjust the cylindrical twin power pack. "Feels secure?" he asked.

Greenie spun around, speaking. "Yes. Thank you. Who are you?"

"Simon-Knight."

Greenie Beanie Jeanie gawked at an athletic Dwarf Man. His cheeks and face were clean-shaven. He had a head full of curly hair and a single ponytail with two knots. He wore a specific type of coat.

"You're country is Khanclover. And that's a Fire Knight Coat, officially called a Phyrecoat because it acts as a shield against the Primordial Element, Phyre. You're a Fire Knight!?" Greenie gasped in shock and dismay. Quickly, she knelt, bowing her head.

"Khanclover is my native country," he said. Raising a brow, noticing her action, he shook his head. "Miss, you do that for Queens and Kings, and Princesses and Princes. I am neither and none!" Simon-Knight teased. "I am ranked as Essential-Knight," he added.

"Why are you on Zerth 2023?" Greenie asked. "Are you from the famous Fire Knight Academy on earth 34567?" The next question came right on top of the first.

Simon-Knight chuckled.

"Are you with your Troop attending the Spirit of Seven Cowboys, parade, Essential-Knight?" Greenie asked, rising to her feet and realising they were nearly the same height. "I am four feet five inches and sizing you up, Essential-Knight, my best guess, you are five feet and three inches," she remarked.

"Absolutely. Absolutely to all of the above," Simon-Knight replied with a chortle.

"The parade is fun. You can get your face painted, and you can taste some delicious food, spicy or mild. There are various pasta meals with lamb meat slices, buttered or sauteed. My Mom makes great pasta with lamb. There are desserts, cakes, jam or honey squares and more variant foods. Some food comes as far away as the surrounding villages in Village Zone," Greenie explained.

"Shhhhh," Simon-Knight said, raising a finger to his lips.

"Are you with a Fire Knight Troop? Can I meet your friends?"

"The Troop of fruitcakes are at a Seven Saloon getting happy."

"Oh! I am underage to go inside a Seven Saloon. But why do you call your friends fruitcakes? Do they enjoy nutty food?"

Simon-Knight gestured to Greenie's utility. He eyed her with suspicion but in a fun manner. "Are you planning to become a Fire Knight with that belt? And what is the Gizmo attached to it?"

Greenie tilted her head left and then right, working out the kinks, or perhaps it was just a habit. She sized up her new friend, not the least afraid of him; sometimes men can play games and be deceiving in their intentions. Sniffing the air, for the first time, she could smell his attractive cologne. "I created my utility belt because I hope to become a person like you, to help people. People need all over help; homeless people exist all over the Multiverse. I read the Multiverse Newspaper, and my Dad has a subscription, it arrives every Soondee by way of an Inter-dimensional Drone and plops it on our doorstep. My Mom is a physician running a countryside care house, the Jeanie Homestead Long Term Care. My Mom is not Zerth; she originates from Moonsteep, a former Street Surgeon, but my Father is full-blood Zerth. And my Dad is a full-time Zerth, farmer, at the Jeanie Ranch. And this Gizmo," Greenie said, taking off, and the clamp made a *snap* sound. "This is the official Digital School All-Educational Device, and that's a mouthful; just call it, The Homework Device," she explained, watching Simon-Knight withdraw a similar device.

Simon-Knight nodded, listening to the girl yak-yak. It was in his experience girls may tend to yak-yak a little more than boys. He tried not to laugh, but something of a sound slipped out of his lips. He continued to be playfully comparing devices like Best Buds, showing off new fishing tackle or hardware stuff. "This is a Fire Knight All-Purpose Tool. It helps me find locations, but it's not up-linked to any satellite. It has several Mahagick Apps. You will forgive me if I don't share too many details. And I use it as a communication device and other things. Often I fight it, it often doesn't function," he admitted. Greenie snatched it out of his hand.

"Mister Essential-Knight, allow me to re-boot your device." Greenie turned it on and then examined the symbols along the right and left sides. She nodded, sizing up the issues. Next, Greenie began typing the universal Multiverse keyboard at lightspeed with two fingers. "*My Mom taught me how to read and write in the Multiverse Key Symbols*," she thought. Simon-Knight blinked. The screen blinked off for ten seconds and then came back on. "Mister Simon-Knight, I reset your systems; they were tangled up in knots. Your All-Purpose Device was no doubt knocked about during fantastic battles, and so the knocking about jumbled up systems, slowing down the CPU process system. The AI was obviously given a shake-and-bake syndrome or whatever," Greenie explained, handing it back.

He thoughtfully rubbed his clean-shaven chin. He made a facial expression, thinking. "How did you come to that conclusion?" Simon-Knight asked.

Greenie shrugged. She made a hand gesture to her head. "It's all upstairs, uuuhh, just the way I understand things. My nutty brain!" she teased and released a giggle. "I am guessing your All-Purpose Fire Knight Device has Zilohertz Crystals that are able to up-link to the global energy planetary grid," she said.

"One would need to be nutty to belong to the Fire Knight Troop," Simon-Knight explained and provoked a giggle from the girl. "I gather you are on the way home. Well, have a good flight," he said.

"How are your adventures?" she asked. "I would think your adventures are fun," she added.

"Adventures, you call them adventures," Simon-Knight said with a small smile, "Missy, to become a Fire Knight, one must realise it's a serious business. We are not seeking fortune or prize money from a lottery. Fire Knights are Multiverse knights, we attend school as children and teenagers and as adults. We are classified as Superheroes because of Gene-Thirteen. It's not adventures we seek, and we actively bring harmony and balance when darkness grows too powerful. The Battle of Taprobane Island verse Arezon-Knysght and his legions of Phyre Creatures is an example. Go home to your family," Simon-Knight insisted. "Be Humble and allow the Great Spirit to Bless You," he added.

Greenie soon lifted off the ground as the thrusters pushed down. The fire the jet pack created was Mahagick, blue and magically would not burn people. It had the power to allow a person to fly.

Simon-Knight Part 2

(Invincible, Two Steps From Hell)

Gazing skyward, Simon-Knight watched a flock of long body, oval-winged birds with long beaks fly over Spirit of Seven Cowboys. The eyes were crystal red, fire red. They were Zerth Mothmirds. The flock of Mothmirds adjusted their path, flying away toward the old city, Zomeople City.

"Old City... Zomeople City, Fire Knight will be creeping through the Zomeople City, gathering intelligence. A brouhaha of whispers engages our ears, something about the return of the Amemga and stealing souls for the purpose of enslavement. Enslavement is not a good investment nor a good adventure, and a Fire Knight does not prosper only a tyrant. The Zomeople of Zerth, a strange species indeed because they don't interact with people. Humph!

Adventures, so that's what young people conceive in their youthful sea of imagination. HUMPH!... My mentor trained me to understand my objects were to aide those who require assistance but always beware of those who may invent some instrument that may do more harm than good. A good battle to defeat an evil inventor is worth the blood spilt, but the buckets of blood spilt can never be truly tolerated. My mentor taught me that the less blood spilt, the less weight on our shoulders and soul. I am not without a conscious; anger doesn't brew in my stomach, I don't hunger for battle, but I am prepared for battle.

Fire Knight Academy is my training ground, a palace perched on a rock connected to the mainland by a suspension bridge. Earth 34567, Canamerica, a country of good and corrupt, a country *compassionate but determined never to be second, and a country home to Abraham State, where Fire Knight Academy is located. The school contains as many as three thousand teenagers spanning the Twelve Zodiac Multiverses, and the teenagers are Classified as Superhero because of a gene. The supernaturals are Murians, humanoids, and the Cat Race. There are other Academies in other Multiverses and so the Fire Knight people are an open society, better or worse, but many graduates go on to contribute to society as a whole. Johnny Vlogger is a Fire Knight, a good friend and a man who has travelled extensively on Zerth.*

Humph!

Adventures that's the topic for this thinking process. Fire Knights solve mysteries, we are investigators, we hunt, and we ambush targets only those attempting to cause chaos and disturbances of vast proportions. And we drastically failed to protect the citizens of a country called America on what has become a catchphrase, Nine-Eleven. We failed to prevent the Pearl Harbor disaster. America of earth 23123, a world I won't easily forget. But, we did not fail to help the Americans build a device to stop what they called the First World War. Five rockets carried the devices, and they were dropped on the Nazi continent, destroying the manufacturing factories. We were able to avert the disgusting cleansing of a whole nation controlled by a powerful army, the Nazis, although many did die. The body count could have been much worse. The American nation of earth 34567 rose to each challenge with our assistance, and that included squaring off with Adolf Azzenhole. If one were to call war an adventure, I have a second opinion—a bloody mess.

The Fire Knights have helped America on many earth-like worlds, including planet Moonsteep. There is no America on Zerth, and I wonder why that is.

Humph!

It's time to join my colleges at the bar. Two drinks, one for my soul and one for me! And perhaps a third drink before bedtime. Simon-Knight walked off, exiting Seven Park for a saloon.

Flight to Jeanie Ranch

(Flight of the Bumblebee)

The evening glowing golden sunset was a beacon, a candle showing the way home.

Greenie navigated the jet pack using joysticks. They could steer left and right, up or down and straight. The helmet was wirelessly set up, and the face shield showed holographic information, an altimetre, airspeed indicators, an altitude indicator, a horizon situation display and warning panels. "*My world is full of extremes, buggies, blimps, bicycles and Hopperhorses for transportation. EMS vehicles are powered by motors spewing a stew of unsavoury odours. Well, some of the farm equipment is not so great either. But, my jet pack is powered by orange Zilohertz Crystals, Mahagick Power and clean alternative energy.*

Winnykneebee is two years old than me, but our education system allows teens to pick and choose courses they feel will enrich their personal lives. So, students might be older or younger. Our choices of courses range from Mahagick Class, Classic Astronomy, Multiverse Astronomy, History Class, Ancient History Class and Multiverse Class. Sasquiche and share various classes, too. Winnykneebee has real Faith in her culture, Vamphyrism. She would never put me in danger, and she just saved my life, silly me standing in the middle of the street. She and I are a Mahagick Team in class working on projects. The Triplet Sisters, they are fun to hang with, again older; they are always either butting heads with each other or playing pranks on one another or just being sisters, but they are sisters. I don't have any sisters, and I am surprised how relaxed they make me feel with their quirky sense of play. I got an older brother, cousins, uncles and aunts," Greenie continued thinking while navigating across one side of Spirit of Seven Cowboys, which was rich with life, but the opposite side was full of industry smokestacks.

The labyrinth of coal power plants from an aerial view could be solved by seeing the weaving interconnecting pathways. Large rock walls separated whole sections of the path and forced workers to keep in separate zones. *"It's baffling my imagination why there are rock walls. The Zomeoples work within the coal zone,"* Greenie thought. The coal power produced power required eight hundred square kilometres, including Little Village Cowboy Area, consisting of the sprawling farm's neighbourhood. *"I am pretty sure the Farm Neighbourhood is about six hundred farmers, some large and some hobby farms,"* she thought. The odour spewing from the smokestacks was enough to make a person dizzy and disorientated, and was mind-numbing. And it was not difficult to see the labyrinth of stacked cube complexes, the habit zone designated for Zomeoples tucked within a whole separate walled area. *"Never met a Zomeople, but famous Fire Knight Johnny Vlogger has, and according to myth, he married a Zerth girl who became infected with the Zhoul virus and mutated into a Zomeople. That is a tragedy,"* Greenie continued thinking. *"Zomeoples are a different humanoid species,"* she concluded while navigating right.

The forest beneath, Squiggle Trees, Toothy Jaw-Trees, Knotted-Trees and Fang Branch Trees, and Snowflake trees decorated the landscape. The woven tapestry, by nature, took on its own creature shapes when looking upon the forest from an aerial advantage. One image is a flying creature, a second image is a snail and a third is a fish creature, and there were others. And flying over tree tops were a flock of Crimsons, chests of fur-coloured crimson and bony bodies with thin triangular wings.

They had snouts rather than pointy beaks. *"The Crimsons won't attack humans unless they feel threatened,"* Greenie thought and continued to steer deeper, flying further over the forest.

Greenie could see off in the far distance flying vehicles. The face cover of the helmet allowed her to zoom in. *"Lucifer City,"* she thought. The skyscrapers glowed like torches, silently calling people. *"My Uncle, Dad's brother, accompanied by several people, often ventures off to Lucifer City delivering supplies to various businesses,"* she thought. *"Lucifer City, that's exactly where the Multiverse group, Super Assassins, will be playing at the famous Fantasea Dome. They are a super core Great Spirit Group, songs with messages, storytelling and fun lyrics, and I got four cassettes. Winnykneebee, the Triplet Sisters and I, will be going. Winnykneebee told me that while in Seven Park, she won eight tickets after answering skill-testing questions on a Faraway Frequency Radio Show, and a drone delivered the tickets. Neat-oh!"* Greenie thought.

Steering again, adjusting the arm controls, Greenie could see the snaking road parting through the forest. It would go on and on for several kilometres, perhaps four hundred and then forked going into another neighbourhood of farms. Portions of the road were cloaked by the trees. The helmet provided night vision technology, and the screen was a whitish colour. She felt comfortable wearing the two-piece all-weather flight suit and the invigorating late afternoon/evening spring air in Vamphyre.

The holographic timepiece read 5:38 pm.

"Home sweet home!" Greenie said aloud, seeing the farm house glowing. It sat in the middle zone, surrounded by adult Toffee Trees, sixty to seventy metres tall. The trees were ready to bear toffee squares, and within the month of Vamphyre, she would help pick off toffee squares. The Toffee Trees won several awards from the Tree Hugger Corp., the Best Natural Tree Award (2 times), the Sweetest Toffee Award (5 times), Best Trimmed Tree Award (3 times) and the Best Healthy Roots Award (3 Times).

Performing a single circle around the farm, below were the animals in the long weedy Zipper Flowers growing in the meadows. *"The Zipper Flowers don't fully unzip for another three weeks, but when they do open, they are quite big with fuzzy, soft inner tentacles. Don't touch; they don't sting, but the slick oil can burn and give a rash. For whatever reason, I never got a greenish/purple rash. I was nine at the time. Bewilder my imagination,"* she thought. It was too dark to see everything, but she knew where the Jeanie River flowed. The Jeanie Ranch sprawled out, covering fifteen hundred acres. Droids tended to the everyday labour.

She pressed a button on one of the joysticks. It sent a wireless signal, and the landing pad blue light was activated. She activated the landing system and the jet pack manuevered to allow a smooth vertical descent. She felt no tummy knots during the descent, confident but not cocky. Her legs absorbed the bump in a spongy manner, and it did not seem to bother her muscles as though they were superior in design, but then again, Greenie was a country girl, and farming would nurture her bones to be resistant to bumps.

The front door opened. Inner light rushed out, making the immediate surrounding bright. A man and woman emerged, looking toward the landing pad and watching a girl, their daughter, remove the flight gear.

"Greenie is our miracle, Beanie," Maharz said with an arm around his tall Moonsteep, Eknakamoonknoon woman. She stood a slender image but a solid three feet taller than her husband, and

Maharz himself was six feet tall. "She gets the miracle from your Ozone-Soul," he added.

Beanie Greenie Jeanie looked down upon the man she fell in love with, and her smile went from ear to ear.

"You words make my heart quiver," she responded in a hearty, raspy voice, "your words hold me prisoner on this farm. It's a simple life, but we manage. I love you for that, Maharz, so I am going to kiss you!" Beanie leaned over her husband and gave him a suck-face. When the couple separated lips, they exchanged adult giggles. They enjoyed playing games. The clothing she wore was a one-piece, all-blue Street Surgeon uniform with an emblem of a Moonsteep creature as the official medical symbol. It was a winged sphinx with a blue body and a snake coiled around its body. "We're going to invent a new game," she said.

"I will exercise my imagination," Maharz replied and then purposely wiggled his brows.

Greenie approached her parents. Her mother towered over her husband. "Were you just two smooching?"

"Never mind, young lady, your evening platter of nourishment is prepared," Maharz said in a hearty manner, "and how was school today before the long weekend? School was out three hours ago, so your Mother and I had hoped you would have returned quicker. We need to pick off the Toffee Squares. Oh! Don't forget we're picking toffee squares on Soondee morning for the Toffee Festival next weekend within the Farm Neighbourhood," he continued speaking.

"Next weekend is the Toffee Festival?" Greenie asked in surprise. "I thought it was two weeks after the long weekend. Amnesia Effect," she commented, placing a hand on her forehead.

The Jeanie Family

(John Carpenter - HALLOWEEN Theme)

"Greenie, the Toffee Festival comes the following long weekend," Beanie said, leading the group inside the house through the vestibule and around the corner, the living room area and kitchen. "Do not ever imagine you are using the Amnesia Effect; you are much too young," she teased.

Time stopped for Greenie. She stood staring at her family as though they were the exterior of her realm. Suddenly, her body wrapped around them, performing a perfect 360 and plunking her back in the exact spot. During the wraparound, she could see their shapely shadows stretch thin, becoming silhouette skeletonised images and a river of red drink.

"What is matter?" Maharz asked, stepping forward and placing fatherly palms resting upon her shoulder. "Do you need assistance removing the rocket pack?" he continued, asking questions.

A kiss of winter cool air blew against the girl's face, awakening her, and her nose twitched.

Greenie wiggled out of the knapsack, letting it drop and smoothly catching it mid-fall. Items inside the bag clanked. "Let me change and shower before sitting," she remarked. Her mind quickly closed up the dreadful dream so she would not remember. "I need to check on Corkey-Dorkey, clean his cage," she said. Purposely, she stuck out her tongue at her older brother sitting at the table, and he exchanged greetings with the baby finger and index finger. "*At least Aarat knows who the boss is; we have a mutual understanding,*" she thought. "*The word Aarat comes from the Great Spirit Book, the name of secret mountain, keeper of the lost Ark on Taprobane Island,*" she continued thinking while slipping off the shoe boots using the toe of one shoe and then her bare foot toes.

"Phew!" Aarat snapped in response waving his hand, teasing. "Don't your toes get warts or red dots?" he asked.

"Never. Never ever, no warts?"

Greenie made had gestures. "Never, never ever, no warts. I don't catch colds either, nor do I get infected by allergies," she said to her big brother, watching his frown.

"We can wait an hour for you to freshen up," Maharz said with a clap of his hands as a final word.

The tubular bath tub lifted Greenie out. It was called an Elevator-Tub. She stepped onto the bathmat and reached for the big bath towel. She wrapped it around her body. "*Mom knows I am different than most Zerth girls, but I still get my periods once every three months as typical Zerth girls. Yeccc! It will be three months; just finished a week ago. It cost me two days of school. Yeccc! Winnykneebee asked about my period because we're going to Lucifer City to watch the Super Assassins; Winnykneebee was just being nosy in a girlish manner.*

Mom knows I am different because I am a hybrid of Moonsteep genes and Zerth genes. But, Aarat doesn't understand just how strange my body is and not because I am a girl shifting toward womanhood, the secrets I possess about my abilities, and perhaps more than even I fully understand," Greenie thought, looking at the reflection of herself in the bathroom mirror. "*I hope that my inner oddities won't scare aware Sasquiche; I like him, Great Spirit and sincerely believe Sasquiche would make good for a future companion. Don't let me lose Sasquiche, Great Spirit,"* she prayed inwardly and turning away she stepped toward the bathroom door, and it slid open, responding to sensing body heat.

Greenie and Beanie

(God Part II, U2)

Stepping from the washroom, Greenie entered her bedroom. Lingering in the air was an inviting odour. The scented candle burned in a safe place. It sat inside a safety transparent container with an opening at the top. She stared at the flame, admiring the flicker as it appeared to dance on the spot, a strange and eerie tango. It captivated her imagination, and somehow she reflected on the 'amber' of the cigarette butt when that Dude flicked away the butt. The amber burned a bright red.

She deliberately went about the room touching knickknacks, crystals, bracelets, and a coloured square she could play with by twisting sides and matching all the sides into single colours.

Panning her head left, set up in a specific spacious area a large table had a whole farm. It contained farm creatures, Featherhorses, Hopperhorses, Cheetah-Hump, and humming Lyrical-Lynx and grunting, grudging Jumper-Pigs. Stepping over to the farm modelling table, she carefully lifted the top of the barn made of thin modelling sticks. Inside, it showed a detailed architecture structure. To achieve this, Greenie followed instructions images, which included animal stalls for the Horn-Cow, Leopard-Goats with tucks, and Wolf-Chickens.

On the opposite side of the room, a second card table had electrical wires, taken from the influential things of the modern age: Gizmos, Gadgets, Thingamajigs, Whatchamacallits and a Robertson Screwdriver. While the others were taken apart for their parts and pieces, Greenie understood fully that it was the handy-dandy Robertson Screwdriver that gave her the multiverse tools required to complete self-orientated tasks. "*I built my Faraway Frequency Radio using Robertson, carefully screwing tiny screws into the hardboard and then layering it with the wafers and using Gizmo-Glue to keep them from sliding about. It took two weeks to carefully construct my Faraway Frequency Radio, and I'm currently hooked into the Multiverse-Tube, and I listen to frequencies, Multipod shows or music from the Twelve Zodiac Multiverses. Dad and Uncle helped, but they made sure I learned. I am unsure why Uncle called me a genius; I don't feel like one,*" she admitted, thinking. "*It doesn't operate on Quartz; it harnesses the blue, orange and green Zilohertz crystals,*" she continued thinking.

"Greenie, Greenie, Greenie, my best friend is Little Greenie Beanie Jeanie," sang a creature hanging upside-down homemade grip designed for Dumb-Bats. "I dream of something beautiful, and Greenie, my Little Greenie Beanie Jeanie!" the creature sang its song.

"Corkey-Dorkey, what are you doing out of your cage?" she accused. "Did you wiggle the latch and let yourself out for the umpteenth time!" Stretching out her arm, it was a gesture for her pet to drop off the homemade ceiling grip and, spreading open the wings, parachuted onto her arm. The tri-claws gripped her bare skin but never punctured or left a scratch on the skin.

"I love you, Greenie," Corkey-Dorkey said, giving a smile. The ears wiggled continuously and turned left and right, always honing in on various sounds.

"You speak kind words," she replied and smiled, allowing him to snuggle her chin. A single finger rubbed her pet.

A hard knock came at the bedroom door.

"We're ready to eat," Beanie called out and slowly opened the door. "Greenie, are you getting dressed?"

"Corkey-Dorkey was singing to me," she said. "I will change right away." And she opened the closet door, catching the broom handle as it fell out, about to strike her in the forehead. Next, she raised a leg and placed a foot on the Kick-Ball before it could roll out further while still holding the broom. And finally, a very big stuffed creature fell toward her; it was as big as Greenie. She performed a smooth upward body push with her body, and the stuffed toy was sent back inside the closet. And simultaneously, she placed the broom into a slot, and the ball was tapped back and landed perfectly on a weird flat suction up. The ball stayed put! Greenie reached in, grabbed a long, green shirt and closed the door. Slipping on the shirt, she spun around to her Mother, who stood watching the show. The words on the shirt read: Green is Better than Mean!

"Is there anything you wish to speak to me about?" Beanie asked. "Is it about a boy, Sasniche?" she continued.

Corkey-Dorkey flapped his wings. He purposely whooshed around the room and then settled down, upside down on the ceiling Grasp-Bar for his claws.

"Sasquiche Sasniche. Sasniche is his last name. He is a fully bloodline Sasquatch, just like Big Bull and his buds. Big Bull's Dad is a Sheriff of Spirit of Seven Cowboys. You remember Mr Bull, don't you remember, during parent/teacher night? I am hungry. I met a Fire Knight after school," Greenie spilt the beans, yakking away.

"Get dressed and tell your stories at dinner," Beanie said. "And I remember Mr Bull shedding hair when we briefly shook hands."

"Mom, you can be so over dramatic."

Beanie stepped closer and looked down upon the magnificent and beautiful creation from her womb. She remembered giving birth to both offspring underwater, accompanied by Maharz. The first time with Aarat, she experienced some discomfort, but her womb was learning to stretch, and her body of muscles was going through intense situations of becoming a mother. Reflecting on the subtle pain, the memory of the experience seemed to be enjoyable. Water birthing was the Eknakamoonknoon way; the infant slides out of the open womb, and so does the amniotic fluid, and the infant is instantly immersed in a pool of warm water. The water birth does not mentally scar the infant from the initial shock of coldness, born outside water in a maternity room. Water birthing is a medically controlled, caring birth. Maharz cut the umbilical cord with the help of the nursing staff because he wanted to learn.

And when Beanie leaned over Greenie just enough, she formed a quarter U-shape. It could be considered an animated image. Great Spirit blessed her twice with two offspring. She clearly stood several feet taller than her daughter because of her Moonsteep roots; a whole segment of the Eknakmoonknooners were tall and skinny like beans. Belonging to the Moonsteep culture, living and breathing the air, swimming in clean ponds unpolluted by chemicals from warehouses dumping liquid cancer-causing liquid. Forest fires were quickly doused and taken care of by the Moonsteep Forest Eco-Warriors, including Fire Knights. The aircraft on Moonsteep did not spew chem-trails, adding more needless waste into the sky and seeding the clouds with toxic vapours.

She knew its ancient roots with the Great Spirit, how the image of Spirit appeared in a desert to a group of wandering people from the most ancient lands, three of those countries Eknakamoonknoon, Manlantean and Swamp Nation. Her world was called Pangaea by the Great Spirit because the Spirit told those humdrum and unremarkablebackwards people were contacted and given a warning and how to alter the course of a planet. In time, those humdrum and unexceptional people were transformed in a strange way, and they became remarkable and indestructible, forging the first army of surgeons and called themselves, Street Surgeons. The people of Pangaea called the planet Moonsteep, and the world had been blessed with an opportunity to become a Medical Empire and to teach other worlds about 'Body, mind and soul'. *"The root of Moonsteep goes back in time to a point of amnesia, or perhaps the word means something enduring,"* Beanie thought.

"What is twitching in your mind, Little Eggcorn?" Beanie asked, calling her daughter by an affectionate nickname. *"The Eggcorn in Eknakamoonknoon mythology was a gift from the Great Spirit during a second encounter, and myth is somewhat based on an event. Spirit told Fatherseed to go and plant it in good soil and nurture it so one day it would grow and grow and multiply into thousands and tens of thousands of tree, thus creating a sea of leaves and landscape of shade and a place where people could find shelter and build homes. But, the word 'Eggcorn' is a misinterpretation because the true spelling is 'acorn'. One must listen and pay attention, is the lesson,"* she thought.

"Dad is suitable height, but Aarat is lanky and awkward, both legs tied together, but he's funny how he keeps his balance and is very tall like you, but why did Great Spirit make me short?" Greenie crossed her arms and frowned. "I know I am different, Mom, a hybrid of two worlds, Zerth and Moonsteep. But inside me, I truly feel different, but maybe because I am a girl. And you and Dad allow me to truly stretch out my abilities and learn things I like to learn," she added and scratched her head, nervous.

"Great Spirit has a purpose for you, and so you are exactly the height She wishes. You are my Eggcorn or Acorn, compact, but inside you is a lot more than you can imagine. The acorn might be small, but it grows into a mighty tree with enduring roots. Birds, Dumb-Bats and other fowl make their nests in the branches. Trees are important to giving oxygen because they absorb carbon dioxide," Beanie replied with a smile of amusement, sitting next to her Greenie. "We should talk. You tell me stories about your friends, and I enjoy listening," she continued and then, without even thinking, wrapped two arms around her daughter, determined to show her love.

"Could have fooled me, Mom," Greenie challenged, but with a soft tone, not one might assume being a smart-aleck. She wiggled in her Mom's arms.

"You belong to me, Little Eggcorn, and always remember we share two souls, Zerth and Moonsteep. My arms won't release you so easily, so you will be forced to accept me hugging you. Let you in a wee secret," Beanie remarked. "Grandpa and Grandma are coming during the Toffee Festival all the way from Moonsteep. It is there third time visiting Zerth," she added and only then released her daughter.

A big, bright, sunshine smile appeared on Greenie's face.

"I will watch over your Greenie."

Mother and Daughter tilted their heads upward as if looking up at the same time. Great Spirit may be looking upon them, but instead, it was Corkey-Dorkey hanging upside down.

"I will watch over you, Greenie."

"Dumb-Bat, in your home," Greenie insisted.

"Let me hang around; I will be good."

Family Time

Muttmud barked.

"Muttmud, go look-see in your dish, food!" Greenie ordered being firm to the Growler. And quickly, tail wagging, Muttmud hurried off, knowing the girl master would never lie to him.

"How did your counterinsurgent mindset disarm commonsense and therefore conjure the name Muttmud for a Growler?" Aarat asked, speaking with a gravity of words and attempting to force his sister to think. "You possess a feeble mind, like that of a Dumb-Bat!" he jabbed brotherly smart-aleck wit.

Greenie narrowed her brows, picking up on the words. It was now the time to call out the rabble-rouser. She stepped forward, looking up with a face of serious expression. "Better Muttmud, than Dummutt!"

Aarat rolled his eyes; always a comeback, always.

The Jeanie family sat around the round table. Soy milk for the Zerthlings, Almond Milk for the hybrids and Coconut Milk for pure breed Eknakamoonknooners. It was a medical assessment by Beanie to understand her offspring were a hybrid of Zerth and Moonsteep, required during the growing years the best to ensure their immune system would be strong and able to withstand colds and viruses.

The farm produced most of everything they could want, need and/or desire to eat. On the table in bowls and plates were various dishes, cauliccoli and a creamy, tangy liquid off to one side in a smaller cup and buttery asparacumber, and a plate with thin slices of Mam, which was considered a blessed meat because the ham was red and bloody. The Eknakamoonknoon people long ago gave up ham as a daily diet, and because Greenie and Aarat were hybrids, Beanie wanted her offspring to enjoy being blessed by the Great Spirit. The three-inch blue string beans were called Blue Beans, and the other beans were Orange Beans.

The two-hundred-inch micro-thin ITVD mounted on the living room wall was typically locked to the Multicity channel. It had rabbit ears up-linking to the Multiverse of channels, fourteen million and perhaps ones not yet discovered. Maharz liked to keep it tuned to Multicity. The internal had five orange/purple/and yellow Zilohertz crystals. "In the news this evening at this hour, eight-fourteen pm: the Prison Authority has officially told Multiverse Multitube Corp the Madcap family, four men, four brothers and one sister for a total of five Madcap family members have officially escaped from the Madhatter Maximum co-ed facility on the designated prison earth-like planet 43210," the Anchor said reading from a teleprompter.

"Who cares about a bunch of babadumdums," Aarat spat out a comment.

"Aarat, watch your language!"

"Babadumdums is not a legally a swear word, Mom."

"There will be no babadumdum speak during dinner," Beanie insisted, giving an expression of firmness.

"Dad says babadumdum," Greenie volunteered information.

"See! See! The informant is right!" Aarat pointed a finger at his sister. " counterinsurgent mindset!" he hissed.

Maharz cleared his throat. "Ahem! Aarat, at this point you're adrift at sea and by the next age of the moon, your dinghy will flop over, and a giant fish will swallow you whole," he said in a coded language. *"My son knows I served for seventeen years in the Zeus Navy from as early as twelve enlisted and then active duty eighteen to twenty-five. I often speak in the seaman lingo. The expression 'age of the moon' is the interval from one new moon to the next one,"* he thought.

"Daaaad!" Aarat whined.

The news anchor continued speaking, sharing more information. He continued reading without faltering from a teleprompter. "The Madcap crime family made a name for themselves linked to the three assassinations, earth 23456. One assassin murdered President KJF, Knight-Jesus Frankenstein, in a country called America during Gorbachev's Economic reform policies. At the time of the assassination, KJF was running for his third term. The Madcap gave the hired shooter, a Mister Pasty Lee Harvey Oznut, a Mahagick Refile loaded with several Mahagick Bullets from a typical Mahagick Gun. This particular Mahagick Rifle is manufactured in an earth-like word called Italy, and the short form for Interdimensional Trade/American/Ludwig/Yahweh, and the Headquarters is the Pizza Plaza located in Mafioso District. On Zerth, the Spaghetti Embassy is where people do business with Sicily, and the current Ambassador is Mr Freddie Fettuccine Oregano. The current leader of Sicily is Paparazzi Paparazzo, and the Paparazzo family has retained power for the last three hundred and seventeen years. The Paparazzo family is an enduring legacy spotted with allegations, some corruption, some embezzlement, some forgery, igniting a five-year battle and, of course, finger-pointing toward other political parties claiming 'they' ignited some issues. But, the family approved the largest Children's Hospital in Sicily in association with the Moonsteep Medical Empire. It is suspected by spies who attempt to wiggle their way into organized families to disrupt and dismantle families from the inside, and the Madcap is an off chute the Paparazzo Empire."

Sixty seconds later.

Aarat got to his feet, going over to the remote control.

"Put the remote control down quickly before a school of sharks leap out of the sea of imagination," Maharz ordered.

"Daaaad, who cares to listen about a criminal family."

"You know your Father enjoys the evening news," Beanie said.

"The Interdimensional Telecommunication Visionary Device belongs to me and your Mother. Your Grandpa and Grandma on your Mother's side gave it to us for a newly wed gift, and I had told you that before," Maharz said.

Aarat sighed. He flapped his arms, flustered. "Why is the news so important?"

"Sit and eat," Beanie said, gesturing her son back to the table. "If you are not hungry, I can feed your dinner to the organic garbage cleaner, Muttmud," she continued.

"Counterinsurgent mindset," Greenie whispered, grinning at her brother.

Two minutes later.

"The Mural on the living room wall shows several locations of worlds in Mom's Galaxy in the Moonsteep Multiverse,"

Greenie said, sitting at the table opposite her brother. "and it was painted by Grandpa," she added.

"What's your point?" Aarat asked smart-aleck.

"Grandpa and Grandma are coming next week."

Zomeople

Greenie sat upright in bed, back resting against several pillows and legs stretched out with a book in hand. The book report was about the Zomeople race, chapters four, five and six, and the history teacher, Mr Elfant, expected it to be finished by Moonday.

Chapter 4

"Before the new world, there was a world before Zerth, **Pentateuch**, *and Rouge smashed Shadow-Face, sending fragments upon the Pentateuch. The fear of the people during the rain of rocks is something one can only imagine. It created havoc across the globe. Millions and millions died. In our current world, we measure time eight thousand years, and conjecture claims it's been twelve thousand years since the end of the world and now. When the dust settled, a new world was born, Zerth.*

Zomeople... The Zomeople race was born to become the backbone of the Workforce on the continents of Phyre, Zeus, Frost Lands (Arctic, Antarctica), and Ohsheanna. Other countries don't agree or have quasi-laws related to the treatment of Zomeople. They did not originate on Zerth; the Amemga gods delivered them to Zerth as a gift, so the Pumpskin race and Orange/Ivory race can do other types of non-lethal occupations.

Zomeople are able to resist pain, they can breathe smoke and dangerous toxins, the epidermis is resistant to U VB-rays, cannot get melanoma, nor can the skin burn like a deep suntan or blisters, and they are insect-resistant and plant-impervious. Zomeople are naturally super strong, not supernatural, and able to lift (press) as much as an average five tons to as much as twenty tons. They can run long distances without tiring, and the longest recorded distance is an astonishing five-hundred kilometres.

Zomeople are allowed to reproduce, and girls as young as fourteen are plucked out of groups and become technically known as Organic Infant Biological Machines. The womb of a Zom-Girl is different than regular Zerth Females. From fourteen to twenty-five Zom-Girls are expected to reproduce as many as twelve to fifteen offspring to ensure the Zomeople Population remains a healthy quota. The OIBMs don't get attached to the offspring during pregnancy and could not care less about abdicating them to the Zerth Government. Zomeople don't have the same consciousness development as normal people."

BEEP!...BEEP!...BEEP!

Corkey-Dorkey, looking down upon the whole bedroom, watched over Greenie like a protector. Stretching out the wings, the creature parachuted down and landed on a table.

"Going to sleep... Going to sleep... G'd night, my true love."

BEEP!...BEEP!...BEEP!

Greenie peeked over top of the book, spying on Corkey-Dorkey.

Sasquiche Sasniche

Greenie took her eyes off the immediate page, seeing a green light flashing on the Yak-Yak Box sitting next to her. She moved her brows in a curious manner. Reaching out for the Yak-Yak-Box, she flipped open the cover. Upon opening, it made an audible sound. A thumb pressed the circle portion at the top, and the viewer was activated and popping up appeared a six inch all blue 3D image of Sasquiche Sasniche.

"Hi there, Greenie. I know it's late, maybe ten o'clock, but I just wanted to let you know that I will be at the Spirit of Seven Cowboy Parade tomorrow no later than one pm. Get your chores finished ASAP. Why don't you invite Winnykneebee? Big Bull will be at the parade because his Geezer is the Sheriff." Sasquiche stood in his bedroom, bare feet on a wood floor and standing underneath an old fashion hair salon cone shade hair dryer.

Greenie on a Yak-Yak-Box

(With Arms Wide Open, Creed)

Greenie felt an eagerness of vibes to respond. "*Sasquiche is my friend, yeah, a boy, it's not his fault. Great Spirit blessed his Mother to give her a boy, but he is a super duper singer and performed live without fear in front of me, Winnykneebee and her girlfriend, the Triplets. Sasquiche knows no fear,*" she thought, scrambling off the bed and letting the school textbook fall by the wayside. Standing in the centre of the bedroom, Greenie first aimed the Yak-Yak-Box at a small globe on the ceiling and pressed a button. A blue beam whooshed over her connecting to a blue circle of light where she immediately stood. Next, she spoke aloud, "Sasquiche's number. Operator, connect my wireless signal "QW7" symbol... Now, now, now." She purposely repeated the 'now' portion as a trigger code.

The Operator Yakked in monotone. "Connection in sixty seconds... Dial tone... Connection excellent... Location in the Sasquatch Forest one hundred and five kilometres from the Farm Neighbourhood... Answering...Goodbye."

The odours were a mixture of shampoo, air freshener and cool air with the window partially open.

Sasquiche Sasniche stood brushing his teeth. The blue toothpaste foamed at his lips, making him appear rapid. He wore pyjamas with a logo, and he could see the logo reflection in the mirror, but the words in the reflection were backwards: **Ecnad eerT eht oD**. He shrugged. He made faces. He spat out the toothpaste into a sink designed to fit perfectly between the tree branches. After he filled a glass and rinsed, he examined the upper eyeteeth made him resemble a creature. He was not a creature of the forest, a Slugworm, a terrifying Moshskeeduu or a Slobpuss because his people were Sasquatch and resided in the hundreds of tree houses.

Sasquiche's Father, Muddster Sasniche V, inherited the Gothic Tree through the bloodline. It towered fifteen hundred meters, and the base was one mile wide, containing as many as three hundred homes within the web of branches. The whole community was interconnected by the weaving of wooden walk-paths and hand-cranked lifts to various levels. Many of the tree houses were owned by other Sasquiche family members, great-uncles, grandfathers and cousins. Muddster was the Tree Landlord, and naturally, rent flowed to him.

The planet Zerth contained seventy-eight Gothic Trees globally, more than any other known world.

BEEP!...BEEP!...BEEP!

Running into the washroom, the pet Catfish brought the Yak-Yak-Box, holding it inside its mouth. The fin on top of the creature wiggled, showing happiness. It placed its web feet on the wooden step, stood and spat out the device. It sat looking up.

BEEP!...BEEP!...BEEP!

Sasquiche spun around, seeing his pet wiggling its fin. "Good girl, Holly," he said in a happy mood. He reached for the Yak-Yak-Box, but another hand intercepted.

"Who says you could use my communicator, little hair folical?" eighteen-year-old Mogbog demanded with an expression 'if looks could kill'. It was a simple enough nickname. "I need to pay for the bills, Little Hair Folical," he explained.

"Oh! It's my girlfriend, buzzing me." Sasquiche blinked twice. He scrunched a face. "Just because we live in the Ocean Forest doesn't mean we are Neanderthals!" he continued, holding the phone. "King Pyre Phyre has destroyed one hundred thousand hectares of forest to resettle a vast portion of Vamphyre City.

Although Ocean Forest is an ocean of swamps, bogs, rivers, ponds and hidden lakes, it's still a vital resource for all of Zerth," he said with a mouthful. "I am proud to be a Backwoodsman," he added, giving his brother a speech.

"Who?" Mogbog demanded. "How is it you could possibly obtain a girlfriend at your age: you're a grade five student according to Zerth Educational Institute. You're fourteen, and it's impossible for a grade five student to obtain a girl. I am older than you and wiser," he continued to rant.

"Greenie Beanie Jeanie, she's smart and my good friend, ergo, my girlfriend. And I made friends with Winnybeeknee and her girlfriends, the Triplet sisters, at the park across the street from school." Sasquiche snatched the Yak-Yak-Box away and pressed the answer button. A blue six-inch holographic image appeared. "Hi, Greenie!"

"Impossible. You have a girlfriend?" Mogbog burst out laughing, holding his midsection. He hurried out of the washroom, entering a narrow hall. "Hey, hey, Timberwood! Timberwood!" He called for his other brother.

"Here. What is it?" The twenty year old Timberwood brother with a full facial beard and bare arms covered in hair with the exception of his hands. He spoke with a smooth tone.

Mogbog spun around on the ball of heels to a bedroom. His attention turned to a fingernail. He bit down on the fingernail. He saw his brother older sitting at a desk taking a brief pause at his homework. "Get this, Sasquiche claims he has a girlfriend!"

"Excellent!" Timberwood responded. "Mogbog, you are absent-minded because chewing a fingernail is not appropriate. You can use a nail filer," he explained.

"You believe Sasquiche?" Mogbog shook his head in disbelief. This was not what he expected. "You're always preaching, so stop it!" he barked.

Timberwood swung the chair around, but remained seated. He stared at his younger brother, irked by the prickly response. He combed his fingers through his thick hair, draping over his ears. He was still wearing a school bow tie. "My suggestions have worked for our little Fuzzy Brother!" the twenty-year-old brother said without bragging. He used an appropriate nickname. "Fuzzy Brother came to me a few weeks ago, perhaps twelve weeks ago and told me all about this girl he liked. I wrote down some ideas for him, and from time to time, we talk," Timberwood explained. "Now, if you will excuse me, I need to study for medical exams. I am submitting my papers to the Moonsteep Medical Empire. I am planning on becoming a physician," he added.

"I can't score with Maggie 'The Mystic'!" Mogbog fumed and bewildered. He rambled. "My nightmares are not nightmares; they are lovemares, beautiful images of a surf. I fantasise about Maggie 'The Mystic'. We score on a sunset beach under a wonderful sunny sky. A few birds are circling overhead. The waves crashing upon our naked bodies are cool. We score on a boat --."

"None of that 'scoring' talk in my home. Rudeness," Mrs Beatrice Sasniche scolded, standing in the hall adjacent to a suite bedroom designed for parents. It came with a bathroom. Her clean-shaven face had a thin lather of cool skin cream and curlers flopped in her hair. She also had a beard, as many Sasquatch women do and tied in a knot, showing other males she was a wife and not to make forward advances. It was the males of the species who trimmed their beards so as not to be mistaken for a woman! "Quiet your tonsils, or tie your tongue in a knot; it's your choice. Have you bothered to take the trash cans out, they don't have legs, and so you will need your Sasquatch muscles. Don't shove your chores onto Sasquiche. He washed the dinner dishes. And your sister, Holly, is now going to sleep," she continued, stepping closer.

Sasquiche ran out of the bathroom as if on cue, with the pet Catfish following. "Mom! Mom!" he called excitedly for attention, holding the Yak-Yak-Device. "Greenie's Mom and Dad want to speak with you. Greenie and I want to meet up at the Spirit of Seven Cowboy Parade," he said without being breathless. He handed Mogbog's phone. It showed a holographic image of Mr and Mrs Jeanie.

"My wireless bill will be through the tree top of this Tree House!"

"You are melodramatic," Muddster spoke while sitting in the living room watching Sasquatch Sports. He shifted the recliner around. Rising to his feet, he went over to his wife, paying attention to what was happening.

"Mrs Beanie Jeanie... Beanie... It's Sasquiche's Mother, Beatrice. And how are you and Maharz.... Are we playing Creature Bridge... Muddster is eager to play cards soon... Your parents are coming to visit.... We should all play Creature Bridge... Some of Greenie's cousins might be accompanying your parents from Moonsteep... Sounds like an adventure Greenie... She is such a sweet girl, and Sasquiche is completely hypnotized... Great Spirit writes about Teen Spirit in the Book called Teen Nation."

Fifteen minutes Beatrice and her husband, Muddster, and Sasquiche's younger siblings gathered in the family room. The big Yak-Yak Speaker was set up. Sasquiche held a microphone facing his family and began to sing the lyrics of a rock instrumental song for the sole purpose of entertaining his family, and they listened.

Green's Song Chapter -3-

Life can change so quickly without warning.

Greenie, poor Greenie Beanie Jeanie, no one would dream of such a dreadful moment.

Should it take a bomb to shake you out of your safety zone?

Should it take a tornado to bring the community together?

Should it take an earthquake under your feet to wake you up?

Should it take an invasion to bring countries together?

Life can change so quickly without warning.

Greenie, poor Greenie Beanie Jeanie, no one would dream of such a dreadful moment. Greenie Beanie Jeanie arrived home that evening, and Greenie Beanie Jeanie discovered madness in her home Corkey-Dorkey was missing, and she began searching for her pet, scared he would be so alone. Opening her parent's bedroom, she found Mom and Dad in bed. They were underneath the sheets asleep. Greenie Beanie Jeanie's hand reached out and pulled back the blanket.

"Mom, Dad, Corkey-Dorkey is missing,"

A bloodcurdling scream came like a city siren

A Spiritual Place

(2001 Space Odyssey, Richard Strauss)

The lush landscape of rolling green hills dotted by glossy ponds. It was a beautiful dreamscape.

Trees of every kind, red spruce, oaks, western hemlock, redwoods and other ones, tall, fat, thin, squiggle trees, toothy trees and trees that could walk and talk. The walking trees waded through the Isthmus, and adult trees piggy-backed baby trees. The infant trees produced sounds indicating they were scared of the water but held onto their parent for security.

Tree limbs sway as though they were hands waving, and leaves quiver.

A sky of so blue it would appear to be an ocean overhead and the clouds painted as the waves.

The air carried distinct odours—the fragrance spectrum, acrid, damp, fetid and malodorous. The breeze stirred the odours, washing it across the plains where creatures gathered in herds.

The creatures were of every size imaginable, and they responded to one another in various throaty grunts and snarls and hoot tones.

Ascending over three larger hills and rising, an all-white marble temple was constructed in the middle of the largest of all plains, with only two trees, one on either side of the temple. The marble ceiling was held up by a hundred columns, and some had faces engraved. Behind the temple stood foreboding ice-capped mountains called Spirit. A sparkling glacial lake was at the base of the Spirit Mountain. A pair of whales leapt out of the rolled-over in midair before splashing down. A shining star hovered over the top of the mountain peaks.

In a portion of the blue sky appeared a swirling pooling of stars, but a closer inspection peering through a telescope, each of those stars was individual multiverses. The multiverses were like grains of sand on a groomed beach, each one distinct and all of them containing lifeforms.

A million of Dumb-Bats flew through the sky, a frolic nature. They created a fabric in the sky like a Dumb-Bat afghan blanket.

Everyone bird imaginable flew about the freedom of a sky uninterrupted by winged machines.

The apparition of the face appeared in the sky, looking up all of creation, and simultaneously, a young girl emerged from the temple in a dress. Gazing at the sky, she tilted her head back, admiring the blue, saw the apparition, and waved, "Hello." Greenie smiled in reply.

The Great Spirit Is Calling

(Youth of the Nation, P.O.D.)

Hard knocking.

If an anesthesiologist had knocked Greenie out, it would be ear-splitting thunder waking her out of a dead sleep. She bolted upright. Her heartbeats were a sledgehammer effect, eyes wide open in shock and horror, and throat tightening. She felt a swirl of coldness gripped her skin. And then, for some mysterious reason, she seemed to calm down at limitless speed, her heart returning to a dulcet tempo. Muttmud barked, demanding attention. Voices came from the exterior closed bedroom door, sounds on the floor, her parents were moving about, and she saw the hall light seeping through the cracks in the door. The light became as bright as fire.

"Wrinkle my dreams, ruffle my wings; something strange is upon us," Corkey-Dorkey sang out. He sat on a swing inside the cage.

"Melodramatic," Greenie said, swung her legs over the bedside and stood up with a spring in her knees. She snapped her fingers twice, and the desk lamp sensory honed in on the snap and triggered the system. The Mahagick Bulb went 'on'. Inside the bulb, a single blue crystal glowed as amber at first and grew brighter until the light filled the room.

Hard knocking returned.

"Somebody must be at the front door, Corkey-Dorkey," Greenie assumed. "Take a grip of my arm, and don't play games," she added, opening the cage door. The pet obeyed, squeezing its claws on her bare skin. She felt nothing, not even a pinch.

"Beanie!"

"Farmsmith," Maharz said with a concerned expression, "sit, sit. Sit in the living room," he recommended.

"Forgive me. I know nothing about medicine. My kids are sick—high fever. I really need your assistance, Beanie, please. I know you are a Moonsteep Medic. I often refuse your help, and my family uses Doc Reptile," Farmsmith yammered.

"Of course, you are forgiven!" Beanie remarked, nodding in response. "Take me back to your ranch, and let me see you kids," she urged. "Doc Reptile is a good person, but I am glad you had the Hopperhorses to come to me," she added, seeing her daughter come into the living room.

"Mom. Dad. Hello, Mr Tumbleseed. Is everyone okay?" she asked in an innocent tone. Corkey-Dorkey sat perched now perched on Greenie's shoulder.

"Greenie, go quickly to my lab and fetch me my Moonsteep Medical Bag while I change," Beanie said.

Maharz looked around and saw Aarat standing with bedhead hair and groggy.

"Can I go back to bed?" he asked. "I was sleeping, dreaming about knocking on the door. Can I go back to bed?" he repeated.

"Aarat, this is just a fuzzy dream. Go back to bed," Maharz quipped.

Aarat turned about-face while running his fingers through his hair and returned to his bedroom. The door closed. He fell on the bed.

A lava lamp in the corner of the room glowed, a nightlight!

Greenie ran down a second hall and opened Beanie's Moonsteep Office door and again snapped her fingers and the light came 'on'. Her eyes darted around the office, which contained what appeared to be a file cabinet computer hard drive containing compressed holographic files, and on the floating desk-top, held up by anti-gravity energy, there was a large dark screen HDTV turned off at this moment. It was wirelessly connected to a holographic desk terminal, and gloves sat to one side; Greenie learned how to use it from her Mom.

Further back in the Lab/Office was Mahagick Medical Equiment to help conduct tens of thousands of medical experiments and science experiments. A transparent refrigerator contained petri-dishes, and each one colour-coded. Opening a small closet contained several one-piece Street Surgeon Uniforms and Mahagick Boots with two-inch soles. Greenie could also see three Street Surgeon Utility Belts hanging up on the wrung. A helmet was on the upper shelf.

Behind Greenie was another transparent Moonsteep Omnibiotic Cabinet containing thousands of vials, and each one filled with Smart-Liquid. It was cooled by a separate coolant system.

Greenie spied Beanie's Moonsteep Medical Bag shoved into a nook in the Medical All-Purpose Bed. She grabbed it and rushed out of the door just as Beanie walked inside. They almost collided.

"Can I come, Mom?"

"I need you to learn, always be willing to learn," Beanie responded, cupping her daughter's chin and purposely making eye contact. "I need to change into my Street Surgeon uniform. The

Great is calling, giving me a sensation this home visit may be more serious," she added.

Beanie

(Steve McQueen, Sheryl Crow)

Ten minutes later.

Greenie wore the jet pack. She watched as her Mother came alongside carrying an oval board. They exchanged expressions and a silent conversation.

"Ready, let's soar." Beanie dropped the board, and it floated. Jumping on it, she kept her balance.

Farmsmith rode up on his Featherhorse. He wore an evening riding jacket. He withdrew from a pocket a round hat, but with a simple thumb push it popped into a top hat. He slipped it on and slid a string under his chin, securing it. He gave a nod to the Street Surgeon and Greenie. He gave a gentle spur-kick, encouraging the animal to jump into a dash. It fluttered the wings in a manner to pick up speed, but the animal could not take flight. Its legs moved over the landscape with the velocity of a vehicle pushing sixty kilometres per hour. It would take one hour to reach his farm.

Beanie stood on top of a Mahagick-Board hovering above the ground. It glowed with a purple/ green energy on the underbelly. The Mahagick-Board produced a pleasant humming sound. Adjusting her body she manipulated the board not much different than a surfer.

The standard Mahagick Street Surgeon Goggles helped provide perfect vision in all-weather and night conditions. It was wirelessly controlled and connected to the Street Surgeon Utility Belt Fable Crystal Computer.

Standing in the door frame, Maharz watched his wife and daughter go off on an adventure. He smiled. He was happy that his daughter had a good relationship with his Beanie.

Greenie could feel the invigorating cool air brushing against her face although she wore the helmet. *"Mom is an excellent Airsurfer. She showed me awards she earned while much younger and living in her home world, Moonsteep. She won the Moonager Surfer Award a staggering four years in a row, making a World Record. She would ride huge waves taller than any man-made skyscraper. She also competed in the Manlantean Surfer Award, coming in second place for three years in a row, beaten each time by a Moonsteep Manlantean named Atlantean Plato. Mom says they even became roommates for a season while at Hammurabi Medical University. Their relationship never got beyond platonic; he never showed interest, always more interested in hanging out with another male friend. Hmmmph! Sounds strange to me. Oh! But, Atlantean and his male friend took my Mom out on her birthday; that was sure swell of them. And, Atlantean provided a shoulder to cry on when Mom broke up with a guy, a Moonsteep dude, who got a little rough, so she told me that story. She shared some stories from her past, which I assume are learning lessons. The guy was charged and spent time in detention; I don't have more information on that subject. Mom told me Atlantean and his male friend both graduated earning a degree in Moonsteep Law and became Moonsteep Medical Officers with the powers of arrest: they pursue criminals who would attempt to use medicine as a weapon. Anyway, I am pretty sure the ocean water would be cold while Airsurfing, but Mom is brave. Mom showed me pictures of her Moonager years, her hair was longer back then and tied up in a wrapped bun. It's neat when Mom encourages me to learn new things, and Dad supports my goals, helping me build my Faraway Frequency Radio so I can listen to music from other*

Multiverses. I like watching Fire Knight adventures of Johnny Vlogger Show and the places he travels, specifically on Zerth.

Johnny Vlogger is from earth 34567 born in the Kitty Hawk State. He resided at the famous Fire Knight Castle and was classified as a Superhero because of gene thirteen. He is not macho dude; he's not overly muscular, and he looks ordinary. He wears bionic goggles to see because he is blind. I guess he could go for an eyeball exchange through the Moonsteep Medical Empire, but he doesn't seem interested. He got married to a Zerth girl. Yes!. Very cool! The Johnny Vlogger Show is always shown live stream with him on duty as a Fire Knight. He can battle creatures and dangerous people and always uses various things, including the Fire Knight Evergreen Phyresword. It's powered by purple Zilohertz crystals. It's a device that can actually retard the primordial phlame, called Phyre. In short, the Evergreen Phyresword is purposely designed so the weird phlame can actually put Phyre out, not to be confused with ordinary fire," Greenie thought while juggling her attention span to control the jet pack. She managed to accomplish the tasks with a natural ability.

Farmsmith Tech-Rancho

(Start Me Up, The Rolling Stones)

Greenie could see through the helmet technology of the Farmsmith Technology Ranch or Tech-Ranch with clarity. It contained a field of satellites scanning the night sky for communication from Outer Space and Exotic Space. At least two days every month since the age of twelve she hung around the grounds, strolling about the inner weaving short streets and at first accompanied by one of her parents. Within the fenced compound of two kilometres, it contained a communication centre and community centre, a factory for assembling goods or packaging other items for shipping off across the Zerth Globe and Exotic Space to the multiverse. Five hundred Zomeoples worked and lived on the Farmsmith from what she learned. It had as many two hundred Zerthlings employed, and they lived at the Farmsmith Motel, and there was a school for their children. There was a small regular Fire Station and a staff of five firefighters, not Fire Knights, and one-floor Medical Centre, where Beanie worked three days per week at her choosing, but it also had a regular Zerth physician. The library, laundromat and small shopping plaza were all contained in one building. It was a world-within-a-world, which included twin helipads and a Zeppelin Station. A pair of bright blue panning and crisscrossing spotlights in the night sky indicated where to land.

Adjacent, the Technology Farm was a sprawling vegetable garden of two hundred acres. It grew just about all the scrumptious organic foods. Droids tended the different sectors accompanied by the gardening team. The Farmsmith was vastly different from the Jeanie Ranch.

Greenie made a touchdown while Beanie stopped the Airboard, manipulating her feet and simultaneously pressing a button on the Utility Buckle.

Without Interdimentional Borders

(Birth of a Hero, Two Steps From Hell)

A clap of thunder came soon, followed by sheet lightning. It began to drip, one drop at a time, until the sky opened and spilt rain.

Farmsmith arrived at his Tech-Ranch seven minutes later. Pulling on the reins and steering the Featherhorse, he navigated the animal over to a specific spot. The Featherhorse wiggled as a creature thing to do. A few feathers were shaken loose. The rain was tickling its body. Farmsmith jumped the creature, boots splashing in a puddle. He rushed toward Street Surgeon Beanie and her daughter, Greenie, standing and waiting on the porch and underneath an awning. He twisted the doorknob and pushed it open.

"My wife died due to pregnancy complications, and my youngest is three years old, as you are aware, Beanie. The other two kids are seven and eleven, but you already know all that," he said, leading them through the interior and to a back room. "I should have listened. Doctor Reptile is living in the Prehistoric Generation, and his concoction of vegetable drinks is a means to cure my kids. I am so stupid," he admitted, controlling his emotions. Next, he gestured to his kids lying in bed. "I am doing the best I can as a single Dad with a business to oversee. The business is in my family bloodline; four of my brothers and three cousins work here on the Tech-Ranch," he continued as Beanie rested a hand on his shoulder.

Quickly, Beanie took control, approaching three kids. Removing a handheld device from the Street Surgeon Utility Belt, she held it over the forehead of each child. The screen had colour codes indicating medical issues. It was officially called Mahagick Medical Device or MMD. The pale green/white colour of skin, and touching the forearm underneath the epidermis, there was a liquid, but not blood, something more dangerous. Greenie observed. Their eyes stared, eyelids fluttered, but they continued to stare.

"What is it, Beanie?" Farmsmith asked, reaching out and touching her shoulder with concern.

Beanie shifted her attention toward the youngest of three years and used the MMD again. This time, she pressed a button, punching up a different scanning system, going deeper and penetrating the skin to the blood level. Greenie leaned closer, seeing images on the screen. Beanie allowed her daughter to observe without hesitation. *"Mom told me on Zerth in our bodies, inside our veins, although we bleed rusty colour, sometimes even a watery purple, but inside us is purple blood. We have types of blood, X-blood is the most abundant, followed by Y-blood and third Z-blood. Those three groups are known as positive, but a fourth blood type is XY and mysterious, the XY mixture can allow Zerthlings to intermix with alien races, and biologists have dubbed it 'Mahagick Blood'. This is how come me and Aarat were able to be born from my Mom's womb, Moonsteep blood conjoined with our XY blood type: I am officially XY-Z, and so is my brother,"* Greenie thought.

Beanie handed the MMD over to Greenie, and the daughter nodded. Next, the Street Surgeon withdrew from a slim pocket on the utility a vial containing Omnibiotics, engineered Smart-Liquid. It was one of several pockets containing the liquid. She withdrew a pen-sized device and slipped the vial inside a slot. Pressing the top of the Medipen, the section closed over and then when Beanie pressed down a second time, an indicator turned green.

"Your children have come into contact with Epiderpuss-pocket, a typical sever cold."

"How?" Farmsmith asked. He could feel the drumming of his heartbeats.

"Zomeople," the Bald Brother accused, "maybe. I chased several Zomeople off our Tech Farm a week ago. Maybe a Zomeople infected the kids," the Bald Brother spoke up.

"Epiderpuss-Pocket is a common air-born virus on Zerth, and it can be fatal after seventy-two hours if not treated." Beanie pressed the flat-head of the Medipen and sprayed the liquid on the neck of the two older children and then the infant.

Greenie rubbed her chin in a thoughtful manner hesitant for a moment, but decided to speak. "Zomeople cannot pass on viruses," she said, "I remember reading about that fact."

"Farmsmith, the serum will be effect immediately," Beanie said watching the colouring of the skin on the forearms and chest area. "Tomorrow at five pm I will return to administer a second inoculation, milder, but they are to remain in bed for a solid week," she continued.

"I would like to hang out at the Spirit of Seven Cowboy Parade with Sasquiche and Winnykneebee."

"You can do that, and you have earned that as a reward for being brave, a hero in my eyes," Beanie replied.

"Mom, the infant is coughing," Greenie said, scared.

"Hemmily; her name is Hemmily," a second Brother said with an assertive tone. The long goatee had three knots.

Greenie's voice tightened for a moment as her eyes captured the situation, and then her voice became excited. "Mom! Hemmily is reacting to the serum."

"We will need to take Hemmily back to my lab; there, I possess an incubator to further analyse her blood," Beanie said.

"Mom, we only have the Airboard and my jet pack."

"How much time do we have?" the third Brother asked, a tattoo-faced man.

"Farmsmith, do you have an infant pack so I can wear it and carry Hemmily to my lab?"

"No."

Greenie snapped her fingers. "Mom! My knapsack." She shook off the knapsack. "Get me a pair of scissors!" she ordered one of the four brothers. Quickly, she started snipping holes in the knapsack for legs, and Beanie picked up on the improvising situation. Beanie picked up Hemmily and slipped the infant inside the knapsack, and the strings secured the infant. "Mom, my jet pack is just as fast as your Airboard. Let me carry Hemmily home, back to the Jeanie Ranch," she requested.

"I will follow," Beanie agreed.

"It's a miracle," the Fourth Brother exclaimed, spreading open his arms. "Great Spirit has blessed our family with so much love," he said and dropped his knees and looked up to the ceiling.

"You will forgive our brother, Edgone; he is our family Pastor," Farmsmith said. "And he does get emotional during intense situations. He is a good man, strange, but he is our Pastor. Shields all of us from sinning," he continued.

The Brother with the knotted beard helped his brother back to his feet, making way for the Mother and Daughter to leave.

"I will follow on my Featherhorse," Farmsmith said.

Thunder boomed in a strange rhythm, the lightning flashed and the environment whooshed as Great Spirit had set forth a celestial rock opera.

"We will bring Hemmily home," Greenie remarked, standing outside dressed in the jet pack with the infant Hemmily on her chest inside the knapsack.

"What Grade are you taking this year?" the Pastor Brother asked.

"Grade Five."

"Well, that explains everything," the Tattoo-Faced Brother said, trying to be witty.

"Winnykneebee, Sasquiche and Me are enrolled in Mr Elfant's History Class."

Spirit of Seven Cowboys

(I am Not A Hero, Batman – The Dark Knight -- Hans Zimmer)

Parade music spilt a delightful spell upon the crowd.

Greenie tilted her head up hearing screeching, but not horrible hellfire screeching, but a flock of Red-Breast Screecher-Owls circled over Park Seven across from the school. They performed some oddball, but graceful bird ritual. *"Great Spirit created birds to keep us looking up at the celestial apron with those Sparkling Galaxies,"* she mused.

Sasquiche noticed Greenie was wearing a student Street Surgeon Blue Cape snapped to the shoulder grippers.

"What fun and intense last night was helping Mr Tumbleseed. Flying Hemmily back home to the Jeanie Ranch tucked into my knapsack," Greenie thought, strolling from the locker zone toward a picnic table accompanied by Sasquiche and Winnykneebee and the Triplets.

"That cape is you!" Doublegum, said one of the Triplet Sisters, and the sisters giggled, amused.

Greenie's expression became suspicious for a moment. "What's so funny about me wearing a cape? On my Mom's planet, Moonsteep, the Street Surgeons use the cape as part of their missions as they move from universe to universe to help worlds that require medical care," she explained. "My Mom is kind of nurturing me to learn about the ways of the Street Surgeon, to help others in time of need, a caring soldier, a soldier without weapons not to hurt but heal. My Mom has told me stories about how the

Moonsteep Medical Empire invades a whole other world, they come in vast ships, invading yeah, but also playing therapeutic music, drumming, a hypnotic effect, drums that Street Surgeons will march to wage war to save lives on a vast scale. They are often assisted by biological artificial people, the Surgeon Platoon, grown from fetuses and mentally uploaded with vast skills to serve Street Surgeons, shielding them from people who would otherwise cause harm through a method of violence. Violence shadows the Street Surgeon lifestyle. It's not for people with fragile hearts. Babadumdum.

A mere three thousand Street Surgeons deployed on planet Gartharian during both an economic up-evil and a plague. A man named Gorbachev helped re-arrange the economics of Gartharian; he was a wizard at economic reform. Mom engaged in the war to save lives on Gartharia as a Street Surgeon. She belonged to a Street Surgeon Team, comprised of about fifty people and code-named: Squid. Mom told me she worked in the Gartharian City of Hypatia, known for its college and universities, further educating girls in multiverse courses. The Street Surgeons converted two of the gymnasiums into makeshift hospitals," she further explained and received a high-five from Sasquiche. While the back of his hand was hairy, fortunately, his palms were clean. Touching the backside, Sasquiche's hand produced a boyish giggle, and so she stopped. "*A war to save lives zzool*," she thought.

"Great Spirit Book, in the chapter Friends and Foe, there is a verse that says just that expression: a war to save lives is zzool," Sasquiche remarked, rubbing his palms and savouring the verse. "Our King Phyre is obnoxious, waging little skirmishes to keep the Zomeople under his grasp. King Phyre isn't my friend," he continued, and Greenie did not say a word but rather gave her guy friend a strange expression, confused. "Gorbachev is a member of the Celestial Economics, heavily affiliated with the Twelve Zodiac Multiverse Council," he added.

"Babadumdum is a quasi-swear word," Winnykneebee remarked, "but I will accept it as a funny word," she added.

"Truly you are a master of literature, Sasquiche; Great Spirit speaks volumes, 'a war to save lives'," Doublegum commented. "You read widely; it's zzool when a man shows he enjoys books for pleasure," she said in a teasing manner. "What book are you packing in your knapsack? Great Gwen Spirit has a privy council and Gorbachev was/is part of it," she added.

Sasquiche pulled on the slipknot string and reached inside the knapsack, pulling out a book titled **Zomeople and Amemga**.

"Zerth could economic reform," Greenie agreed.

Doublegum leaned against the wooden table top. "You make me think of a hero." Next, she slid across the table two sticks of gum. "You deserve a reward," she added and then blew a bubble and let it pop. A portion of bubble gum landed on her nose and, with a quick lick of her long tongue, snatched back inside her mouth.

It was shorter than a dog's tongue but long enough to do the job. Sasquiche observed the whole action. "Zzool," he burped a comment.

"Hey, that's a zzool thing, to be a hero," Sasquiche said enthusiastically and saw Winnykneebee give a hand gesture to simmer down. He straightened up, shoulders back.

"Very zzool," the Triplet Sisters chimed.

Greenie reacted first, placing hands on hips, unsure about the idea of being labelled a 'hero'. Gradually she beamed a smile, becoming zzool. "Great Spirit teaches not to brag heavily, but I confess I improvised how to carry Hemmily back to the Jeanie-Ranch. I turned my knapsack into an infant carry bag. My Street Surgeon Mom helped Hemmily in her private lab," she explained, seeing the Triplet Sisters exchange high-fives in their own weird way of showing approval.

A breath of wind entered Seven Park. Branches of Squiggle Trees began to sway as if pushed carefully by an affectionate hand, not attempting to snap a branch, and the alphabet leaves made a percussion sound. A group of Skunsquirrels stopped chattering among themselves and stood still, but their heads panned left and right in a curious manner as though they were searching for a predator but saw no one. The fur over their body stood up, but not in fear; they felt tingling, and then they rolled over onto their back, exposing their bellies and enjoying a playful moment.

Slithermunks squirming through the blades of tall patches of blue grass raised their fat heads, seeing their natural friends, Skunsquirrels. Rarely would a Skunsquirrel become a predator. Each of the Slithermunks felt a spiritual finger touch their heads, and their ears wiggled in response.

The breath of wind kissed both cheeks of Greenie softly. The breath of wind sent a tingling against Greenie's bare arms. The cape fluttered and then whooshed, spreading open and filling with life, and she reacted by standing up as if summoned to duty.

"Babadumdum! Did any of you feel the breeze give a kiss?" Greenie asked startled. "Babadumdum!" she exclaimed and, while standing, performed a swaying manoeuvre as if dancing on the spot. Her friends observed with a curiousness.

"See, that's the kind of adventure I am encouraging our little group to do," Winnykneebee said, sitting in between the Triplet Sisters. She wore the cultural symbols from the Vamphyre culture, painted a tattoo on her bicep and a necklace with a skeleton head. She was scribbling down everything Greenie was telling her, making official documentation in a diary. "Greenie, if you don't mind, I am going to publish your adventure in the Winnykneebee Newspaper and distribute it throughout the school. I am charging ten cents a copy because I don't give anything away for free," she remarked and received a nod. "Oh, no babadumdum! My Dad says ladies should not be saying babadumdum," she added.

Greenie shook her head in surprise. Perhaps it was a little exaggerated but required to get her mind focused. "You have a newspaper?"

Winnykneebee wigged her groomed and long. "Now I do. You have given me something to publish." Winnykneebee grinned. "My Papa has a photocopier, and I can make copies on it, so long as I have my own paper," she continued.

"What does the money return to?" Sasquiche asked.

"All money earned will be put into an account inspiring my business opportunities, which all of us shall benefit."

"Photographer," Rumblegum said, raising a hand.

"Photographer's assistant," Bubblegum said, raising a hand.

"Do-Girl," Doublegum said, giving a thumbs up and giggled.

"Okay, enough business, let's go enjoy the festivities --."

Simultaneously all their Yak-Yak Boxes played various musical notes demanding attention.

"Parents," they chimed, and each one answered the call.

"Oh, I almost forgot," Winnykneebee said while clicking the 'off' button on the phone. Placing a hand on Greenie's shoulder for a moment, a friendship touch. "The Super Assassin concert at Lucifer City has been pushed back a week due to issues that the promoters are keeping to themselves. Keep the tickets, and they will be honoured," she continued.

Madcap Family

(A Criminal Mind, Gowan – Strange Animal)

The four Madcap brothers wore retardant advanced-type suits complete with face shield helmets. Aiming Mahagick Pistols and squeezing the trigger, squirt streams of Phyre spew out and not to be confused with ordinary fire, a cool cousin on the Primordial Elementary Chart. *"When it comes to the end of the world, Phyre's spirit will move onward across the celestial plain of souls, unfettered by Great Spirit, and arrive at another world to infest like Phyreflyes and conquer,"* Emberg Madcap thought, eldest of the brothers. *"I am a follower of Phyre's Teachings, Book of Phyre found inside the Great Spirit Book: Eat, Smoke and exhale the body of the Phyrespiryt: Enjoy the warm tingling in your lungs, for that is truly Phyrespiryt inside you: Become a brother and sister of everlasting Phyre and know you are stronger than your cooler cousin, Fire. Keep Phyre in your soul and be born into Phyre Nation,"* he continued thinking while squeezing the Mahagick Pistol trigger and squirting a stream of Phyre.

"Arriving on Zerth three months ago, our family bloodline understood what happened long ago. The asteroid named, Rogue, hammered into the second satellite Shadow-Face Moon. Shadow-Face Moon splintered and fractured due to the powerful celestial punch, sending chunks plunging Zerth, creating massive explosions, wiping out whole populations and changing the landscape forever. It's unfortunately what happened to the Pentateuch as this world was known. A new world grew out of the old world known as the Pentateuch, and it evolved, becoming renamed Zerth. Great Spirit wrote about Zerth inside her Great Spirit Book. It can be spooky when an unknown and mysterious Entity has such power sight of future events, including people and

places. No one really knows what the Great Spirit looks like, cloaked in mystery and face protected by a hoodie. And our Madcap Bloodline were one-time Multiverse Map Makers; our ancestors were teachers and adventures and history junkies and thieves for knowledge. Bloodlines matter; blood is the river that gives our anatomy oxygen. No one wants to spill blood. Our family once owned a large amount of land on Zerth, in and around Spirit of Seven Cowboys, long ago, but reclaiming land will spill blood.

The Great Spirit Book has several books between the front and back cover, one specifically called the Book of Phyre. My goal is to always possess in my soul the Phyrespirit. It focuses on Prince Shadow-Lyght and perhaps the Father of Arezon-Knysght, the former King Baal of Vamphyre City. Every one of these ancient characters has nicknames, and Prince Shadow-Lyght's nickname is Moon-Wolfphyre. People, those of us who follow Phyre's Teaching from the Book of Phyre are disciples of Prince Shadow-Lyght; we are the flock of Moon-Wolfphyre. We share the belief that death is required to succeed, and Mahagick Phyre is our method to bring ordinary people, the peasants, to the slaughter," Emberg thought.

"This torch job should get the attention of the Cowboy Coppers and Fire Fighters attention. Glad we stole these protection gear from the Fire Fighter store," Emberg's youngest brother, Long-Mong, said as sensations of giddiness swept through his bones. "This activity is better than sitting, rotting, my body full of grubby prison food, soggy toast, soggy mashed potatoes, soggy carrots, food for dogs. My face; the hairs on my face scrubby and itchy, beard not even clean enough. Living inside the Madhatter Maximum co-ed facility on prison planet 43210. I felt my mind going funny. Just thinking about the last few years makes my head spin. And the whole exterior is surrounded by a one thousand mile, not kilometre chain link fence caging all of us. Madhatter is built underground, but we are allowed out for up to two hours, but we need to go through for checkpoints as we ride an elevator to the exit zone," he added.

"Prison planet 43210, at least we shared a cell for all those years, Big Brother, but my mind at night, I feel the cold stainless toilet seat on my arse. The tap trickled with icy water. We were at the mercy of our inhuman jailers, and they treated us worse than a dog, a beating once in a while. And the other inmates had their own justice, but your faith in Spirit of Phyre, Book of Phyre, and Prince Shadow-Lyght, we are the flock of Moon-Wolfphyre. We, you, created your own group of Wolfphyres, and they helped us overthrow the Madhatter Guards, allowing our family to escape. The Madcap family is the best. We are invincible. Anyway, my ears still ring, hearing the drip, drip, drip, drip of each drop dripping from the stupid faucet into the grey stainless steel sink," Long-Mong said and watched his Emberg gesture to turn off and holster the Mahagick Pistol.

"We are leaving," Dr. Nitroglycerine Madcap and the third eldest brother said.

"Who be you making decisions, Nitro?" Long-Mong accused, gesturing to Emberg. "He's our leader, and Sister is second in command," he added with a sharp tongue.

"This fire will create the diversion needed."

"Nitro, hear me?"

"Long-Mong, be quiet," Coal snapped a verbal punch.

Emberg cast an expression at his brothers. "*Unless one has three young siblings, just try and imagine being the scapegoat parent,*" Emberg thought. "*Nitroglycerine has a hot seed within *his Ozone-Soul and he spits a lack of emotion toward Long-Mong, aloof social skills. Long-Mong likes to gab; doesn't bother me, it gives me an insight into his mental thinking, but he should control his blithering skills. A single word would be overstimulated. It was me who got Long-Mong a girl and helped him over some frustrating issues, but after a few times, he got the hang of meeting girls. It's Phyre's Teaching from the Book of Phyre that we should assist our young brothers to become a man; misogyny does give a young man the power to overcome a woman. Disciples of Prince Shadow-Lyght, we are the flock of Moon-Wolfphyre therefore we are brothers.*

And then there is this thing called the Ozone-Soul and how we're all connected to Great Spirit through sharing a tiny part of her Ozone-Soul. Prince Shadow-Lyght teaches we all separate souls, and through birth, only then, we become bonded through the bloodline, and there is no such proof we are spiritually connected to the Great Spirit through some intangible umbilical cord. Bloodline is stronger than faith and hope, and that is my belief. We have free rein, we decide what to do, and destiny can be altered by our manipulation with power and our skills," Emberg continued thinking.

"Hey, Bro, I will stop when Emberg says so," Long-Mong retorted.

"You're cruising for a bruising," Nitro replied, aiming the Mahagick Pistol at Long-Mong.

Emberg immediately took long strides toward Nitro without hesitation and snatched the pistol away. He held it behind his back. A thumb pressed the 'off button'. He knew the Mahagick Pistol he did not need to even look. *"Father educated me in various weapons, grilled me actually, so I would always be prepared,"* he thought. Staring through the face shield, he glared at Nitro with disapproval, and although he wanted the weapon, back Emberg blocked his attempts.

"Nitroglycerine, you have a short circuit!" Coal responded, stepping back, startled. "Why would you aim the Mahagick Pistol at poor Long-Mong? He is one us, Madcap, a brother of *Moon-Wolfphyre*! And he is your brother and mine!" Coal scolded.

The crackle of fire raged around the Madcap family of brothers.

"Time to go," Long-Mong suggested, seeing walls bleeding with sap and chips of paint.

"This tower will become a burning candle," Emberg admitted and gestured to follow him, which the three brothers obeyed.

Spirit of Seven Cowboys

(Der Koniggratzer March)

Upbeat parade music designed to make audiences young and old happy played.

Greenie Beanie Jeanie sat outside the restaurant accompanied by Sasquiche, Winnykneebee and the Triplet sisters. The adults sat at a table arranged so all the families could be together. The restaurant was called **Salavamp/Vamphyre**, in honour of their culture. "*Winnykneebee's family owns several franchises. It could be easily recognised with the stylish backward letter 'S' and accompanied by the letter 'V'. The wait staff have large-been girls and are blonde and short shorts, while the dudes are muscular and tall and have blue eyes and are blonde. All the wait staff wear necklaces with a skull head,*" Greenie thought. She looked around, eyes searching. "*Mom is still not here, must be still checking on the Farmsmith Tumbleseed kids,*" she continued thinking, rubbing her chin with an index finger.

Winnykneebee leaned closer to her friend. "Greenie, hopefully, you won't think it's evil of me to speak sinisterly, but long before we were born, it was my Salavamp bloodline who fought on the city streets of Vamphyre. Within the city of Vamphyre, there were seventeen thousand Salavamps out of three million residents. We were the smallest of the Vamphyre Bloodlines. King Pyre Phyre is the most dominant. Go look up Salavamp in a phone directory; we're all related. My Father's bloodline engaged in a street war to engage the rising rebels, the Brown Shirts. We were successful and defeated the rise of the group of men calling themselves Nazis in the election in the landscape Vamphyre. The Nazi Party Leader, Adolf /Azzenhole escaped, however, inside a V-rocket disappearing into the multiverse.

King Pyre Phyre's Father rewarded the Salavamp Bloodline, absorbing an astonishing two thousand into its rank and file. Of course, family members went through re-training exercises to see who was the most fit and their abilities. I am not sure how many were finally decided upon to meet the qualifications. My Salavamp Bloodline does have a quirky edge to it," Winnykneebee said, seeing Greenie's eyes open wide.

"Skelazore," Maharz Jeanie's voice was loud enough that Greenie adjusted her head, seeing her father. "The mix of Salavamp Homemade noodle bread and Homemade Tangy Goop green sauce is like Ragzoom music on my taste buds. The spices do the Disco with my taste buds," he teased.

Skelazore smiled. "So you want some Salavamp Pasta breaded dish?"

"Me and my son, Aarat would."

"Will Beanie be joining us?" Mrs Sasquiche asked.

"Soon, I hope."

"Where is Beanie?" Mrs Salavamp asked.

"Checking on Farmsmith's kids, they were sick," Maharz said. "Greenie helped her Mother last night," he added and gave his daughter a cool gesture by crossing over his thumbs making an X. Greenie responded with the same gesture.

The tall and muscular waiter with blonde hair jotted down the orders while standing on the opposite side of the table. Four wait staff worked the table with smoothness, pouring water from jugs into glasses or purple lemonade. *"Purple lemonade was significant as it was the during the Spirit of Seven Cowboys because it represented Great Spirit's Blessing, the blood within her heart chambers,"* Greenie thought and nodded to the waiter to fill her tall glass. She could smell his inviting cologne.

The Triplet Sisters were served the refreshments, as were Winnykneebee and Sasquiche.

Greenie used hand gestures to speak at this moment, perhaps exaggerating her emotions. "And why would you imagine I would be irked by what your bloodline performed to help quash the Nazis. Great Spirit blessed your family to recognise sinister evil characters, and although Adolf escaped in a rocket into the multiverse, may he run out of fuel and hitchhike all the way to somewhere where it's very cold," Greenie remarked.

"The defeat of the Nazi Party in Vamphyre City was thirty-five years ago," Sasquiche spoke up, sitting on Greenie's left. "Adolf escaped in the V-rocket after escaping his jail cell by using a form of hypnosis on three of the guards. According to conjecture, his voice is the superhero power; Adolf lulled the guards to open his cell door and then ordered them to escort him out of jail. He ordered one guard to strip, and he put on the guard's clothes and instructed him to re-enter the prison and lock himself inside the cell. The other two guards drove Adolf to a special place in the Vamphyre Forest, where he met up with loyal men; I am keeping the story simple: and then ordered those two jailers to shoot themselves in the head. No witnesses," Sasquiche explained a simple version of history.

Greenie's attention turned upward suddenly, and she watched several dozen coloured balloons floating higher and higher into the sky. A mix of winged fowls also appeared. A Zeppelin was approaching the township of Spirit of Seven Cowboys. It passed high enough over a smokey tower. She scratched her head, puzzled.

"What was the name of the secret place in the forest Adolf hid the V-Rocket he escaped in?" Bubblegum asked, encouraging him to reveal more.

"Moon Wolfphyre. The building was a shack in the thick Vamphyre Forest, but the engineers had built an underground cold and damp bunker connected to a maze of tunnels to confuse anyone who was not authorised to be there. Adolf lived in the secret bunker dry and clean second bunker for three days with his wife, a mysterious blond woman name Virilian. The Nazis Party Leadership invented a story, taking advantage of the Lore of Vamphyre Forest. They claimed the woods were haunted by the angry Spirit-Sasquatch," Sasquiche explained.

"You really like to read," Doublegum said and giggled. "Moon Wolfphyre originates from the Great Spirit Book," she added, and her sisters nodded.

"The V for the V-Rocket originated from the 'V' in Vamphyre Forest," Rumblegum said as the Spirit of Seven Cowboy's Heartthrob Marching Band started marching by. The fifteen-piece band played a happy-go-lucky song from a bygone era and, although associated with an evil period in life in the Province of Arezon and the capital city, Vamphyre. The battle against the rising Nazi Party and Adolf.

Former Street Surgeon Beanie arrived at the Salavamp Restaurant riding the Airboard. A foot stomp turned off the Airboard thrusters. She hopped off. Maharz leaned over the railing, sharing a hug; he could not wait. The friends laughed and playfully applauded. Greenie could see her mom was clad in the three-piece uniform and wearing the utility belt and cape. She lashed the Airboard secure post. It floated, producing a low melody.

"A hobby," Sasquiche replied, giving an innocent shrug. "My older brother, Timberwood, is studying for exams; he has the brains to become a Moonsteep Surgeon and encourages me. My other brother, Mogbog, thinks I am a pest," he added.

"That's not true, Little Hair Folical," Mogbog said loud enough, sitting two seats away, "you are you, Sasquiche, and you often play games to get attention," he remarked and then growled with a mean expression, but the girls burst out laughing at him.

Sasquiche blinked twice. He scrunched a face. "Just because we live in the Ocean Forest doesn't mean we are Neanderthals!" he continued, holding the phone. "King Pyre Phyre has destroyed one hundred thousand hectares of forest to resettle a vast portion of Vamphyre City. Although Ocean Forest is an ocean of swamps, bogs, rivers, ponds and hidden lakes, it's still a vital resource for all of Zerth," he said with a mouthful. "I am proud to be a Backwoodsman," he added, giving his brother a speech.

"You really have memorized your speech," Doublegum accused and giggled, amused.

"Babadumdum!"

(Bring Me to Life, Evanescence)

"Only my Bloodline has the ears to hear me or the chosen, Greenie," Great Spirit spoke, and she responded, sitting up startled. Her eyes darted around, seeing friends and family. No one seemed to notice her actions. *"It is time for you to wake up and recognise your true purpose, and your life will unfold, taking you on a sweeping multiverse journey. Inside you is the heart soul-rock; his name is Rogue and as my Bloodline, you have inherited his name as faith and enduring strength. You will be unstoppable as a rogue asteroid. You will pack a powerful punch. Your foot speed will be that of a rogue asteroid, and thus, nothing mortal-made will be able to throw you off balance: a head-on collision with a train will not stop you. You may slip or leap off from the top of the highest mountain and land on the ground, shaking the world like a child's rattle, but your legs will never be broken or your body. You will be able to prepare yourself at a limitless speed. You will have the strength of the God-Creature, Zooclaw, Lord of all Beasts on Zerth. Creatures will obey you; some may attempt to test, but they will only fail. Ordinary fire will never scar your skin, nor will Primordial Element, Phyre. Remember these words.... Be humble... Be Patient...Be willing to learn... Be you and... Don't be someone you are not... Now, go and begin your journey,"* Great Spirit encouraged.

A breath of wind kissed both cheeks of Greenie softly. The breath of wind tingled Greenie's bare arms. The cape fluttered and then whooshed, spreading open and filling with life, and she reacted by standing up as if summoned to duty.

"Babadumdum! Did any of you feel the breeze give a kiss?" Greenie asked startled. "Babadumdum!" she exclaimed and, while standing, performed a swaying manoeuvre as if dancing on the spot. Her friends observed with a curiousness.

All the adults turned their attention toward Greenie.

The parade participants, some clad in colourful costumes, flags boasting the Spirit of Seven Cowboys, decorated floats, banners and signs attached to vehicles and people on horseback, including a Fire Knight Troop. Greenie spotted Simon-Knight riding on a horse.

Choices We Make, To Fight Fate

(Linkin Park - In The End)

"Ms Jeanie," a man in a charcoal suit said. "I am King Pyre Phyre's Royal attache. You may call me Mister Stingray," he continued.

"Greenie, sit down and stop acting like a child!" Maharz scolded.

"Was a bug biting your butt?" Mogbog asked teasing.

"Whoa," Greenie replied, placing a hand on her forehead. Sasquiche quickly responded, stood up and helped his friend back in the chair. "It's the same emotion, Sasquiche, I felt at the park," she whispered to him, and he nodded.

Winnykneebee nodded at Sasquiche approvingly.

The Triplet Sisters smiled at Sasquiche. The young man had certainly come in handy.

"I am Beanie, Greenie's Mother," she answered Mr Stingray.

Mister Stingray raised a brow both curiously and surprised. "You look like a person from Moonsteep."

Beanie rubbed her chin, thinking before speaking. "I am Moonsteep. Eknakamoonknoon is my Tribe, but not everyone is my height because some of my Tribe can shape-shift the epidermis and create faces. I represent the segment of my Eknakamoonknoon people. I am a former Street Surgeon affiliated with the Moonsteep Medical Empire. This is my husband, Maharz Jeanie of Zerth, and the current heir/owner of Jeanie Ranch. My son, Aarat. My daughter, Greenie." Beanie had no issue speaking proudly about her Moonsteep Tribe or being a mother of a family.

Maharz stood up, reaching out an arm, shaking Mr Stingray's hand and purposely making eye contact, a farmer's attitude when meeting a stranger.

"And what brings the King's Attache to the Salavamp Restaurant?" Mr Salavamp asked. "It's not for sale, but I can offer a franchise," he joked.

"I am here to hand over an invitation, a letter requesting Ms Greenie Beanie Jeanie to a birthday party along with one thousand secretly selected guests by King Pyre Phyre. Greenie shares the same birthday," he explained, handing the letter out, but Beanie snatched it away.

"Mom, the letter was meant for me!"

Beanie hesitated to open the letter. She decided to hand it to Greenie.

The Invitation

Dear Ms Greenie Beanie Jeanie,

Hip-Trip Be-Pop!

I am King Pyre Phyre of the country Zeus. You are invited to spend a weekend with me and one thousand others who share my birth date. Arrangements will be made for transportation and return home to your family at the cost of the state. Looking forward to meeting you.

Cordially, King Pyre Phyre.

The Towering Inferno

(Slip to the Void, Alter Bridge)

KAAAAA-BOOM!

The parade of dance troops and cheerleaders with colourful large pom-poms gave a brief performance and received a cheer. The acrobats were walking on hands ,and the upside clowns—a military formation filed by. Suddenly, everyone stopped and stood still, frozen in a moment in time.

Greenie stood up again, and this time with thunder on her feet. She pointed toward the towering inferno. "Mom! Mom! People will be trapped inside; we need to help trapped people. You can use the Street Surgeon Airboard."

Mr Stingray's jaw dropped in horror and shock.

Patrons on the patio watched with curiousness and concern.

"Our Father is a Spirit of Seven Cowboy Fire Fighter," Bubblegum blurted. "Dad is on duty today, but he did say he would drop by. Our Mother is with us," she added, speaking in a spit-and-spatter blither, trying to be calm.

"Fifteen years a Fire Fighter," Doublegum remarked as she felt Bubblegum take hold of her hand and squeeze it. Doublegum squeezed back, a sisterly squeeze. "Bubblegum, relax, Dad is a capable Fire Fighter. Great Spirit shields people who do good deeds. He would never put himself in danger," she said with a soothing tone. "Grandpa was also a Fire Fighter like our Great Grandpa and before Great Grandpa. Our entire bloodline is full of Fire Fighters, and our two older brothers are attending Fire

School," she continued. "I am going to become the first girl Fire Fighter," she concluded.

The Triplet Brothers, sitting flanking either side of their Mother, turned their attention toward their sisters at that moment and smiled. "Fire Fighters!" The Brother with speckles on his nose got up and went over to Bubblegum and shared a hug while the other brother stayed next to his Mom.

"The Spirit of Seven Cowboys Fire Fighters are part of our socioeconomic fabric success," Winnykneebee spoke up.

"Dad has a Fire Knight Troop staying at our family motel currently, pals," Rumblegum said. Next, she placed a hand on Bubblegum's shoulder for reassurance. "I met this tall giant-size Fire Knight, Peter Rock," she continued.

"May the Great Spirit Bless everyone, Ozone-Soul," Mr Salavamp said, standing up in awe and shock.

Greenie did not hesitate, leaping over the railing and picking up the jet pack on the other side. Sasquiche followed. She slipped on the jet pack. Sasquiche helped be sure it was secure. He gave the typical Zerth thumbs X expression.

Beanie jumped over the railing and unlashed the Airboard. She jumped on top.

The Mother and Daughter flew off as friends, staff workers and other patrons watched.

Hundreds of parade spectators watched.

King Pyre Phyre, a photogenic face, clean shaven and standing just outside the Salavamp Restaurant flanked by bodyguards. He turned his attention toward two figures in flight.

A Mother and Daughter

(Hero – Chad Kroeger feat. Josey Scott)

"There was nothing to avoid; no one offered an incentive. My Mom taught me there were issues in life that had significant and binding behaviour, coefficiency and teamwork is the foreseeable future. Co-operation, like the Fire Knights a force to reckon with. There was no emotional distortion, nothing to be confused about; we both understood what we needed to do. If our actions are alien, if our actions seem to be abnormal, a Mother and Daughter, this may be oddball for Zerth, but my Father does encourage Mom to give me all the opportunities my neurons can absorb and retain. As a former Street Surgeon, it's a no brainer my Mom would be nurturing me to understand how to behave, the Street Surgeon mindset. This was one of those coefficiency moments, teamwork, facing a towering inferno, watching people smashing furniture at windows busting them open and allowing smoke to billow up the side. Reaching out their arms and shouting for help to escape being burned to death, consumed by fire," Greenie thought as she navigated closer to the smoking inferno. She could see through the face shield a father holding a child and begging her to get closer. She nodded. She manoeuvred closer and turned around where the knapsack was located. "My knapsack has foot holes," Greenie shouted.

The Father caught on, slipped his child inside and used a belt to secure the child.

Greenie could feel the ruffling about as she hovered. "*Do not fret. Your jet pack is fully capable of hovering; it's powered by Zilohertz. Be calm, although I am twenty stories above the ground. Be calm. Great Spirit will know you are helping rescue a child, and so the Spirit won't let you fail,"* she continued thinking. It was taking time; it felt like a long time, but then she felt a hand tap her shoulder. She flew forward, taking a spiral descent to the parade below. A police officer rushed up as if on cue, removing the crying and scared child from the knapsack.

Beanie navigated the Airboard smoothly. She caught sight of her daughter hovering five floors above. She arrived at a balcony. The front of the Airboard extended forward and became wider and flat fat. She gestured, showing four fingers, and all four residents carefully climbed over the railing and sat down, crossing their legs. Beanie swerved away and took riders to a park below, and they slid off. Beanie manipulated her feet, and the Airboard backed up and then lifted vertically and flew back to the burning inferno.

Greenie arrived at another floor, ignoring the hot smoke, and for a second time, was able to rescue a child. The knapsack was re-used. *"Great Spirit writes in her Book: People do things because they can, they possess a reptilian tongue, people do things because they are evil, those types of people are deceptive and manipulative, taking advantage of people who are perhaps mentally vulnerable, which I learned in Mind Mental Class, but people also do things because their actions are governed by Great Spirit, and the nurturing of a mentor. People can often do things that perhaps are absurd, preposterous."*

Residences were oozing out of the ground floor escape puffs of black smoke.

The Madcap family were in a lot behind the building; their buggy was under arms under a tree. They climbed inside while Emberg's sister went up top, taking the reins to the two Hopperhorses.

Sirens screamed as fire trucks and crews; they belonged to the Spirit of Seven Cowboys EMS.

Five Fatcopters swarmed over the smokey and fiery scene and hovered. The blades produced a whooshing sound. The Helivatiator, sitting within a transparent bubble, pressed a row of buttons on the dashboard, activating the sprinkler system. The cylindrical tank underneath began spraying water above the skyscraper. The Fatcopters were deliberately designed for battles, creating rain and drenching the exterior.

The Fire Fighters within the passenger zone dressed like guerrilla soldiers but in firefighter uniforms, grasped the handles of a Fire Cannon. Squeezing the trigger, the cannon released hundreds of large marbles. They exploded, releasing retardant energy and splattering against the exterior, ambushing the fire. The Father of the Triplet Sisters performed his duty with a badass laugh, "Come to Papa!"

A Sheriff and Son

(Dance With the Devil, Breaking Benjamin)

Fifteen minutes ago

Fire Knight Troop 1812, all eight members cranked their heads upon hearing the explosion. They watched in shock and disbelief as a plume of black smoke rose while they were mounted on horses. The skyscraper became a towering candle of fire.

A flock of Wingfoxes resting on top of the building whooshed up, releasing terrifying screeches. They scattered like pigeons. The fire captured several Wingfoxes lathering their wings into fire and consumed them. Those Wingfoxes became like tiny shooting stars until they fell and died. The creatures were not much bigger than pigeons. Bully, Sasquiche's school friend, looked up and saw a falling flaming Wingfox, and he jumped out of the path. It dropped near his feet, charred. The creatures were not much bigger than pigeons.

Immediately, Troop Leader Knever Kneeler's horse reared on his hind legs and released an outcry. Quickly, she took control and, with a soothing tone, calmed the horse.

"Northumberland, your behaviour surprises," Knever Kneeler said, reaching forward and with a palm smoothed his main, "perhaps all this parade attention has overdosed your battle-strong heart and iron will with beautiful warmth. People do love you, Northumberland, just like me, because you are a handsome and majestic blue stallion," she continued playing a typical game and ensuring she trusted him as he trusted her. And Northumberland replied with a friendly grunt and two nods.

"Fire Knight Troop, we are in a fire battle," Peter Rock shouted.

"Horse Team, take us to our Fire Cycles," Simon-Knight ordered in a hearty voice. "Ung-jagung-hoop-zung-da-lala!" He said, using a Mahagick word. *"Mahagick Class during my younger years gave me the opportunity to attend Mahagick Church, and the rewards are as a gourmet meal,"* Simon-Knight thought.

The eight horses understood the word. It was Northumberland giving a mighty whinny as a command. The other seven horses returned horse sounds in agreement. They stood still as a swirling energy flickered around at first. A rainbow of Mahagick ringlets whooshed out of the thing air. With primordial powers as a collective, the team transformed into winged horses.

Peter Rock shouted. "Fly, oh mighty winged creatures!"

Bully heard the shouts standing among the crowd. He ran into a crowded street and started shouting repeatedly. "Clear a path for the horses!" And his Father, one of the Sheriffs of Spirit of Seven Cowboys, his attention turned to his son and saw him making gestures to clear away the people.

"Son! Son!" Sheriff shouted, "I am coming to help." He gestured to fellow officers to follow. A law enforcement Father and Son aided by an officer helped to clear a path for the Fire Knight horses as they began galloping, and in only a few steps, the wings opened the horses took flight.

The Fire Knights

(Fire Knight Song, Super Assassins)

Chapter One – Great Spirit Diary Rock Psalm 5

We are Fire Knights for the Great Spirit, our Master Chief

We did not choose to go to war, but everyone has the power of choice

In our DNA is a warrior, the flesh for the Great Spirit

Life can be snuffed out like a single guitar riff

The Great Spirit of life put the war in our DNA, our ozone-soul

We did not choose to go to war, but everyone has the power of choice

You choose to live or die, you choose your fight, and you choose to kill

Our hearts long for peace as our lips hunger for a simple kiss

The Great Spirit gave us the power; protect the innocent with our actions and as words soft as kisses

Words are swords

(Whisper Voice) We are not alone....

Two more Fatcopters dumped water over the fiery apartment.

The winged horses, Northumberland in the lead position, flew, flapping powerful wings over the landscape. They trotted across airspace with the grace of birds. Simon-Knight looked down for a few seconds, his eyes seeing pastures as irregular shapes and creatures, a herd of wild Hopperhorses and Featherhorse galloping across the sprawling openness. The Farm Neighbourhood yawned far and wide, perhaps a world within a world, certainly the breadbasket of the country of Phyre. *"One riding upon a winged horse has the blessings of Great Spirit, for the rider and horse are one-entity. 'There is no divide between the rider and winged horse',"* he thought, thinking of a Great Spirit Verse.

"The Land of Normans has such a beautiful landscape, just like the country of Phyre, but it took many generations to sculpt the soil, tame it and teach it to allow seeds for planting and irrigation concepts. Our landscape originally was much too rough. The Land of Normans is the largest Zone, as the parliament members define vast areas, in my country of Khanclover. Eight blocks of groomed beaches wrapped around a portion of Khanclover. I remember fondly helping a dozen men put a beached Hornwhale back into the Zerth Sea. Hhhhmmmm. Upon approaching the Zerth Sea, from the land, one will see giant boulders left behind from the annihilation of our moon, Shadow-Face. My home town of Zagamagatagazaga is the capital town of Khanclover adjacent to the capitol city Khan," he continued thinking.

Chapter Two – Great Spirit Diary Rock Psalm 5

Our blood is neither alkaline nor is it acidic.

Our blood is addicted to this battle, a rattle and hum; Oh hear the thunder drum.

We are Fire Knights for the Great Spirit, our Master Chief

It makes no common sense to stand on the front line, bodies hanging on a clothesline

We did not choose to go to war, but everyone has the power of choice

You choose to live or die, you choose your fight, and you choose to kill

We are not jarheads, we are not dead, but we will soak your heart in dread

We do not lie, but our brothers and sisters lay scattered on battlefields

We are not jarheads, we are not dead, but we will soak your heart in dread

We are not grunts, we are not runts, but we will shunt bodies off the battlefields

The exoskeleton masks the human inside; no warrior is invisible except the Great Spirit...

(Whisper voice) We are not alone

Ahead, Simon-Knight could see rising out of the Amemga Forest a mountain with a flat top. It was as though Great Spirit had purposely sliced off the peak in one smooth stroke, leaving it smooth. *"The ancient Zerth Tribe of the old world Pentateuch, the Nayam arrived shortly afterwards and built dozens and dozens of stone structures all across the planet, according to paleo-archaeologists. I remember my school year studying about the Nayam Tribe. Their gods supposedly were the Amemga Race, but never proven they existed. The Nayam Tribe also were responsible for building the natural stone castle on top of the Emmaga Mountain located in the Amemga Forest,"* Simon-Knight continued thinking while navigating his winged horse. She released sounds.

"Be well, be happy, Merkaba," he said in a confident tone, leaning slightly forward, "you are always in good hands. I sense you need a wee bit of reminding, a secret game you play on me and enjoy. I enjoy speaking with you. A Dwarf will always treat your species with respect. I will kiss you before I set out for the next battle. Our race has been blessed to have your race as friends," Simon-Knight continued and released a gleeful laugh. He could see below a mountain rising out of the forest. "Currently, we are fetching the Fire Cycles. Long ago, your species' bravery was our reward for battling the creature Phyre, but now we use machines. It's for your protection," he said.

The horses were given a gentle tug, steering them down. Peter Rock gave a verbal command to his horse. All the winged horses spiralled down with a smoothness, gliding, and one by one, landed outside a stone castle. There was a grassy groomed runway designed for them and for unique Fire Knight vehicles.

"Archer-Knight Zandra Sunknife open the door," Knever-Kneeler said, giving a gesture. Archer-Knight Zandar Sunknife, the Teenage Fire Knight, nodded. The youthful round face gave an innocent appearance, and no matter how she tried to be serious, there was a girlish smile at this stage of her life. Archer-Knight official age was classified as Twenteeteen, according to the measurement of time on planet Pearl. She saw the dirty strawberry hair, remarkable like herself, perhaps a coincidence Great Spirit had given Knever-Kneeler a picture of herself. Knever-Kneeler understood and replied with a motherish smile, a gift to the young girl she decided to mentor. *"Zandra is an orphan from earth-like world 54321, a world at war verse the Adolf Army and the Synopath race is affiliated. Madness! I found Zandra in an orphanage operated by child slave tyrants. More madness! She is my orphan, and I will share with her all of my fire battle knowledge. My Fire Knight Troop 1812 rescued three hundred alien children from across the Twelve Zodiac Multiverses and burned the orphanage to the ground. Those Nazi criminals, pirates and sex abusers are rotting in jail, but some chose to commit suicide, cheating prosecution. Zandra is my spark,"* Knever-Kneeler thought.

Zandra dismounted. Brush hair out of her face; her fingers could feel the stringiness, and it needed to be washed. She made a throaty sound, irritated by the feel of her hair. When it was clean, it had a bounce to it, and she liked that feeling. Approaching the double oval twelve-foot tall doors, she whistled a melody. The Mahagick melody frequency activated gears behind the doors causing them to open with smoothness. Turning around with a quickness, no meandering about at this point, Zandra remounted the horse and followed the others inside the courtyard. She was the youngest of the Troop 1812.

Quickly, several workers affiliated with the Fire Knight Community rushed over to the horses as the riders dismounted.

"Master-Tech, are the Fire Cycles ready for flight and battle?" Master Fire Knight Knever Kneeler asked, her voice reasonably brisk. "Our time is short. It has taken us seven minutes to travel from Spirit of Seven Cowboys to the Fire Knight Forte," she added.

"Yes," he replied.

One Troop member produced a grunge throat sound, attracting attention. "All of us should have gone into battle with our majestic horses," Garhawk spoke in a natural croaky tone as most Gartharian's do. She stood six and a half feet tall, and her body was naturally wrestler-fit as Gartharian race is. "Great Spirit was wise to bless the winged horses for the purpose of fighting the Element Phyre," she continued.

"And what would you suggest the horse won't be put in the way of danger?" Peter Rock argued.

"Great Spirit gave these creatures a purpose; machines take that away," Garhawk said, stepping forward. She showed an aggressive nature as a positive thing for a Gartharian woman. Peter Rock stood his full height of seven feet three inches and looked down at the friend and teammate.

"Garhawk, Peter Rock, we all change in the Fire Cycle Garage," Knever Kneeler ordered, snapping her fingers. "Eight minutes have slipped by, and those Fatcopters do not possess our Mahagick Liquid to combat Phyre," she said.

Each Fire Knight changed, stripping from the parade costumes and into flexible battle-tech clothes. Each one slipped on the utility belt equipped with various tools and devices to confront challenges during the fire, and they were not hunting for Easter Eggs. They wore Mahagick two-inch sole boots capable of retarding fire and primordial Element Phyre. And lastly as they each raced out of the garage, the Master Tech handed each one the

Evergreen Phyresword. He hollered in an encouraging manner, "Fire Knights, hopscotch! Trout Sherrout, you're always the last!"

The Moonsteep Manlantean man was fashionably dressed, wearing the Sea-Suit, and his head sheltered by an upside fish bowl.

"I am enlisted as Street Surgeon to care for Fire Knights during battle," Trout replied. "I never imagined an assignment would bring me to planet Zerth," he added.

"Save the 'Home-Free Save-the-Bunch-Speech' for another time," Master-Tech said.

"Fire Fighting can be playing Hide-and-Seek when searching for bodies," Trout replied sharply.

"Eleven minutes!" Knever-Kneeler shouted, mounting the cherry-coloured Fire Cycle. The moment she sat, the systems ignited. The console lit up with several colours. "No one here is impressing me, blow wind upskirt," she said, although she had never worn a skirt in her entire life.

"You, wearing a skirt?" Simon-Knight asked, raising a brow.

"Figure of speech, Dwarf!"

The Fire Knights
Part Two

(Fire Knight Song, Super Assassins)

Chapter Three: Great Spirit Diary Rock Psalm 5

Our hearts long for peace as lips hunger for a simple kiss

The Great Spirit gave us the choice; protect the innocent with our actions and words soft as kisses

Words are swords, the doors to our thoughts that cannot be bought

Evolution leads to revolution, illusion, delusion, optical conclusion

Our salvation through this war is through our actions and words

And words are swords, the doors to our thoughts that cannot be bought

We are Fire Knights for the Great Spirit, our Master Chief

Our blood is addicted to this battle, a rattle and hum; Oh hear the thunder drum

It makes no common sense to stand on the front line, bodies hanging on a clothesline

We did not choose to go to war, but everyone has the power of choice

You choose to live or die, you choose your fight, and you choose to kill

The Great Spirit of life put the war in our DNA, our Ozone-Soul

A Phyre Battle

(Slip to the Void, Alter Bridge)

Fire Knight Troop 1812 navigated Fire Cycles, soaring at an altitude of ten thousand feet. The Fire Knight Cycles were aerodynamic streamlined vehicles with a total of four wheels outstretched like wings, and the wheels transformed into superior fans spinning at a blinding velocity to help keep balance. The Zilohertz purple, orange and green crystals adapted to the Zerth supernatural Keylines soaking up inexhaustible resourceful energy. The riders' bodies stretched flat rather than upright, keeping themselves underneath the wind.

Simon-Knight glanced at the Zilodometer, seeing the needle was steadfast at double OH point seven. *"Only a century ago, Fire Knights used the winged horse fleet to battle the primordial element Phyre or regular fire, but Mahagick Member Tom Blaze changed all that with his invention of the flying Fire Cycle. In the last forty years, there has been an aggressive push to market the Fire Cycles to other Fire Knight Forte within the Twelve Multiverses. Tom has a daughter, Bianca Blaze, enrolled in the Fire Knight Academy on earth 34567 in the country Canamerica. Tom and his wife invited me to a feat at their estate, and members of Troop 1812 were welcomed,"* Simon-Knight continued thinking.

Greenie Beanie Jeanie crashed against the railing of a balcony. She gasped, shocked. *"Bewilder my imagination!"* she thought. The people hoping to escape the smoke retreated. It was an awkward manoeuvre to land on the balcony. The impact jarred the right jet pack cylindrical exhaust. *"Now what?"* she continued thinking as her mind raced with concern. Looking at the visor screen, an alarm began beeping, indicating system 'of line'. "*Give me a sign, Great Spirit,*" she thought, pressing the re-ignition button several times as the left compensated for thirty seconds before shutting off. The jet pack whirled her in a complete circle. Greenie decided to hit the quick release and allowed the jet pack to drop away, free-falling to the ground. Simultaneously, before gravity could grab her, she leapt forward, clearing the railing and landing squarely on her feet, surprising the people. "Great Spirit, thanks for the push!" Greenie said.

"Shalloween-Scream!" the Father exclaimed, shocked by the action. He spoke a personal expression. "What's your plan?" the Father asked.

"My Mother gave me a snap-on Street Surgeon Mahagick cape," Greenie explained. "Yuck! I can taste the smoke even with my Mahagick Helmet. What floor is this?"

"Twelfth floor," the Mother said, cradling her infant as a crying seven-year-old hugged her Father's leg.

Greenie reached for the utility belt. "My Mom has been teaching me how to use the Street Surgeon tools. Hold on. We don't have much time."

"Tell me something I don't know," the Father replied sarcastically while watching as the teenage girl whipped out from a pocket a second Mahagick Cape. It grew and grew.

"Wrap the cape around your body; carry the child!"

"What are you suggesting?" the Father asked.

"We're taking the stairwell," Greenie asserted her objective and standing her ground.

"Greenie!" a voice shouted.

"Mom." She could see Beanie standing on the Airboard next to the balcony railing. "This family needs help."

"Everyone, on the front of my Airboard. I can fly all of you down safely," Beanie said.

The family climbed over the railing and sat on the front portion of the Airboard, which was oval flat. Beanie realised there was no more room left for her daughter.

"Stay put on the balcony; I will return ASAP," she instructed.

Fire Knight Troop 1812 arrived on the scene riding the Fire Cycles.

Hundreds of people from Spirit of Seven Cowboys looked up and watched as the action unfolded.

A flock of long body, oval-winged birds with long beaks flew over Spirit of Seven Cowboys. The eyes were crystal red, fire red. They circled the burning inferno like moths drawn to a flame. They were Zerth Mothmirds. The flock of Mothmirds continued circling the inferno, and when someone jumped out, escaping the burning hell, two birds swooped down and snatched the body. Their jaws were able to hold the body of an entire man. Both birds tore the body, each one taking half. The scream was short. Blood splurt.

"So cool!" Bully said, watching while standing next to his Sheriff Father of Spirit of Seven Cowboys. "But, I hope Greenie is unhurt," he added, looking at his Father's expression.

"Not good!" Sasquiche remarked sitting with friends at the Salavamp Restaurant.

"A sign of dread," Winnykneebee agreed.

"My Sister is the most awesome person on Zerth!"

"I am King Pyre Phyre, you are the brother?"

"Aarat."

"Maharz, Greenie's Father."

King Pyre Phyre, flanked by bodyguards, permitted himself to shake hands, although he wore gloves protecting him from catching germs.

Winnykneebee and the Triplet sisters watched King Pyre Phyre greet the other half of the Jeanie family.

Sasquiche stayed glued to the action, sensing how his heartbeats drummed. He could never imagined knowing someone with such a heroic rock, a toughness to endure.

"Garhawk, activate the Mahagick Water and spray the eastern and western portion," Knever-Kneeler ordered, communicating through a wireless helmet linkup. "Zandra, swing around and cover the north and south sides of this skyscraper. Peter Rock, get to the top of the building and secure it. Manlantean, go with Simon-Knight inside the building a search for people," she continued, giving orders. Nicknames at this point were required, no specific pronouns and so Knever-Kneeler controlled stress through nicknames. Nicknames were fun, and she knew it, knowing Manlantean was a Street Surgeon and associated with the Moonsteep Medical Empire.

A portion of the skyscraper exploded, releasing a bright orange and red fireball. Debris rained upon the ground below and hit some of the escaping residents. The regular firefighters of Spirit of Seven Cowboys scrambled for safety.

Greenie, running through a smokey narrow, pushed by residents as the building was shaking. Her heart raced. Her mind was focused on the thing, *"Great Spirit, give me wings to fly."* She arrived at the stairwell and shoved through the residence, ignoring their irked shouts. Climbing the stairs as people were filing down, people shouting, "You're going the wrong way!"

Beanie watched as the people slid off the Airboard. Next, looking up, her face went ghastly pale. *"What have you done!"* And then she saw the Fire Knight arrive, flying on the fantastic Fire Cycles. Two of the Fire Knights began spraying the exterior of the inferno.

Simon-Knight and Peter Rock set down on the rooftop. Hopping off the Fire Cycles while withdrawing the Mahagick Pistols, they began shooting Mahagick Green Water at the tarred rooftop. Each splat of Mahagick Water released glitter with primordial energy. It had a life of its own, quickly crawling across the tarred roof, keeping it in an extremely Mahagick Cold state so the fire beneath would not be able to ignite.

Simon-Knight approached the roof door to the stairwell; it burst open and out ran a girl he recognised. He had met the girl at Park Seven.

A great quake rattled the rooftop. Flames shot up in pockets where the Mahagick Green Water had not lathered. It had become a Phyre Battle.

Battle Ready

(Birth of a Hero, Two Steps From Hell)

Greenie Beanie Jeanie did not see Simon-Knight or Peter Rock running in the opposite direction toward the edge of the building. She hopped on top of the ledge. Looking down it was a long, long fall.

"Wait!" Simon-Knight shouted.

"Don't jump!" Peter Rock encouraged.

"Hey. It's you. Don't fret. My Mother has prepared me and mentored me to become a Street Surgeon, but I have a dream to become a Fire Knight. This is a Street Surgeon uniform." Greenie turned away and leapt off the edge, bold and fearless.

Beanie watched in shock and dismay, seeing with sharp eye her daughter leap off the top of the inferno.

People gasped in shock at the Salavamp Restaurant.

King Pyre Phyre and his bodyguards were catapulted beyond words, and a great soldier had been born.

"Fetch me that girl!" the King instructed his men.

"Her name is Greenie Beanie Jeanie!" Sasquiche remarked.

"Who are you, her boyfriend?"

"Yeah. I am!"

Winnykneebee and the Triplet Sisters nodded in agreement.

Greenie performed a spectacular midair somersault. Next, she went flat. A hand smacked the utility belt centre button, and the Street Surgeon Cape whooshed, transforming into a parachute. Reaching up, she held the toggles steering the chute. "*A Street Surgeon always comes prepared for battle,*" Greenie thought and landed in Park Seven. The chute/cape dropped behind, draped in a super-heroine fashion.

People approached Park Seven, flooding into it and found the girl who had done something no other Zerthling achieved. She stood in the Street Surgeon Uniform, but the cape gave a profound appearance. The crowd admired and gazed upon the girl. Sasquiche dared to push through the crowd, followed by Winnykneebee and the Triplet Sisters. He was welcomed with open arms and the girlfriends surrounded forming a big hug.

A reporter using an old-fashioned bulb camera, the bulb flashed, capturing a moment of immortality and infamy—a black and white photo of an astonishing girl.

Beanie floated over the crowd and lowered the Airboard. Sliding off the board she approached her daughter.

"Greenie!" she said, awestruck, but then embraced her, a Mother and daughter together and safe.

The News

(Life is a Highway, Tom Cochrane)

Three days later.

A marching band; a hip-hop song.

Phyre News Network filmed the scene with dozens of on-the-ground camera crews.

The Citizens of Spirit of Seven Cowboys filled the main strip celebrating a day to remember the birth of a heroine. A quick banner stretched across the street: **GREENIE BEANIE JEANIE**. A ticker-tate parade, confetti raining and coloured ribbons. A single convertible buggy pulled by a team of Hopperhorses had the Jeanie family riding inside, and a single Backwoods person, Sasquiche Sasniche and Greenie, held his hand. The car behind them carried Winnykneebee and the Triplet Sisters and King Pyre Phyre, and all of them wore big western hats, proud to be here in Spirit of Seven Cowboys. And behind them were the Fire Knights riding upon the winged horses, the Fire Cycles sat in the Fire Knight Fort on top of Emmaga Mountain.

"*It is odd how the girl, Greenie, whom I met in Park Seven, has become such a powerful individual. The citizens of the city are drawn to her like a bee to a ripe flower. Could this child become more than I can imagine? And I am concerned, no... Irked my Fire Knight senses did not buzz me*," Simon-Knight thought, riding Merkaba.

The convertible buggy pulled into a loop lot at City Hall. The Jeanie family climbed out. The City Mayor and Council members were present and decked out in their best uniforms.

"Ladies and Gentlemen of Spirit of Seven Cowboys, welcome the Jeanie Family!" the Mayor said, speaking into the speaker. "A Mother, as you can see, dressed in a Moonsteep Street Surgeon Uniform, and her daughter, Greenie Beanie Jeanie, helped rescue dozens of people, as all of you are aware."

A rousing applause came and shouts of wishes and whistles.

The Madcap family was watching the action unfold while hiding within the crowd.

Greenie received a medallion around her neck for bravery.

Former Street Surgeon Beanie and Mother, she received a medallion. She held Maharz hand and Aarat.

Sasquiche stood next to Greenie, and they held hands while facing thousands of Spirit of Seven Cowboy Citizens. They shared a kiss.

Suddenly, out of the blue, a Dumb-Bat arrived and perched on Greenie's shoulder.

"Corkey-Dorkey! Did you follow us from the farm?"

"I love you, Greenie. You are my best friend!"

"Quiet. Sit and be quiet!"

Corkey-Dorkey responded, nuzzling against her head.

The Spirit of Seven Cowboy Citizens once again gave a rousing applause.

The Jeanie family and Sasquiche were accompanied by King Pyre Phyre and Winnykneebee and the Triplet sisters. The Fire Knights stood behind the Jeanie family.

TO BE CONTINUED

The Super Assassins

Chapter Four: Great Spirit Diary Rock Psalm 5

Great Spirit is our Master Chief

We are Fire Knights for the Great Spirit, our Master Chief

Godbless each battle we fight each night

Ozone-Souls depend on our Spirit of fight and flight

Always remember...

Great Spirit is our Master Chief

Great Spirit is our Master Chief

Great Spirit is our Master Chief

Remember the name, Great Spirit

(Whisper voice) We are not alone....

About the Author

Unfortunately, I don't have any dogs, cats, parrots, rabbits, guinea pigs, penguins, elephants, rhinos or Sabretooth Tigers, nor do I have Lions, Tigers or Bears for pets... And including no worms, slugs, creepy crawlies, weird insects that glow in the dark.... But I know how to use a Typewriter!....

The Smithsonian Institute Department of Ancient Creatures classified this type of typewriter as a Smith Corona. It's an odd-looking creature and can be domesticated. It appeared one day -- poof -- on a sunny beach in California just a short while after the dinosaurs went extinct -65- million years ago!

Milton Keynes UK
Ingram Content Group UK Ltd.
UKHW050131240224
438350UK00006B/51